A
FEW
DAYS
in
MARCH

Published 2012 by BBB

© 2012 D. Thompson

ISBN 978-0-9570623-0-6

ALL PROFITS FROM THIS BOOK WILL BE DONATED TO PARKINSON'S UK.

In aid of

PARKINSON'S UK
CHANGE ATTITUDES.
FIND A CURE.
JOIN US.

Parkinson's UK is the operating name of the Parkinson's Disease Society of the United Kingdom. A charity registered in England and Wales (258197) and in Scotland (SC037554).

Free confidential helpline 0808 800 0303
parkinsons.org.uk
hello@parkinsons.org.uk

Parkinson's UK is the leading Parkinson's support and research charity. They are dedicated to finding a cure and improving life for everyone affected by Parkinson's.

The author would like to thank H. C. who provided the motivation for the novel and N. K. who had the skill to interpret his hand writing.

Designed by April Sky Design www.aprilsky.co.uk

A
FEW
DAYS
in
MARCH

David Thompson

This too shall pass

In memoriam
Robert

CHAPTER 1

The peal of Sunday morning church bells wafted across the bay, gently reminding the faithful of their religious observances, and the rest of the population that it was Sunday, the day of rest, peace and limited licensing hours.

The unusually warm March weather had encouraged winter hibernals to sally forth in force. All season dog walkers with their pooh bags dangling from their wrists like sling shots, found themselves and their canine companions, competing for space on the picturesque coastal path with the early spring's crop of cyclists, power walkers, joggers, skateboarders, pram pushers and the silent killers – the unlicensed, untrained, untested and frequently unskilled, geriatrics on their electric mobility scooters, threatening the lives and limbs of the unwary.

On the man-made lake by the playground, usually occupied by pedalo swans, a group of elderly men sailed beautifully made, radio controlled, model boats of all descriptions, watched by envious boys aged from six to eighty-six.

In the Marina, early season pleasure craft owners were considering the relative merits of putting to sea or simply remaining moored whilst they enjoyed a cup of tea on board.

It was an idyllic day in Bangor.

Originally a late 19th century holiday resort, Bangor was now largely a dormitory town for Belfast, the appeal being good transport links, fine facilities and a superb outlook.

Not surprisingly it was a popular retirement destination,

limited, of course to those who could afford the high property prices.

Such a figure was Mike Wilson, a semi-retired entrepreneur.

Mike was a big man, big in every way. Well over six foot and a solid 200lbs. All his physical attributes were large much to the delight of his numerous female friends. However, it was his bigheartedness and generosity of spirit which really attracted people to him.

How he made his money was a bit of a mystery: actually, it really wasn't, because everyone knew he lived life on the criminal edge and was aware of at least some of his little business schemes. He traded in dubious quality replicas, mostly watches, and would seldom be without a stack of Omega and Rolex time pieces. He had interests in a number of massage parlours – Gentlemen's Clubs – he preferred to call them. A little cannabis was traded now and then and he could always be relied upon to supply alcohol and tobacco from unregulated sources.

His nature was such that no-one begrudged his criminal leanings, in fact his company, noted for its humour and storytelling ability, was often sought at middle class parties where his presence injected a frisson of excitement, even danger into the dull soft lives of his hosts. Mike's views and stories, usually fairly extreme, and his delivery of them, usually very funny, were like a window onto another world. A world they need not enter, but could view with safety.

Of a naturally helpful disposition, if he sometimes stayed later than the other guests and after the host had retired, it was for the purely altruistic reason of helping the hostess with the cleaning up, which included not only filling the dishwasher but also a thorough dusting down of the sofa.

He lived in a prestigious apartment block overlooking the harbour of the North Down coastal town. He liked places with a history, and since the building housing the apartments dated back to the 1890s, his desire for a residence of character was fulfilled. Mind you, behind the façade which, as a listed building, had to be retained, the apartments were ultra modern, but it was the façade, with its large bays and tall windows which determined the internal layout. The rooms were high ceilinged and generously dimensioned, each apartment with its own panoramic view and balcony/patio arrangements for relaxation. Often in the good weather, Mike would sit enjoying the sun and admiring the view, sometimes listening to the radio or simply dozing.

He reckoned the view was to die for. From the town itself with its harbour and Marina, he could scan the Antrim coast across the mouth of Belfast Lough, the Scottish coast from Jura down to the Solway Firth, the Isle of Man, and on a very clear day, even the Lake District peaks.

Living there delighted Mike and gave him a sense of well-being. Originating from the Docks area of Belfast he saw the ownership of his apartment as the achievement of one of his success criteria. The other residents liked him and turned a blind eye to the comings and goings at his apartment, although they did get peeved when delivery vans, carrying God knows what, paid overnight visits, blocking their parking spaces. Strangely, law breaking activities seemed not to worry them, but the temporary loss of a parking space was regarded as a major catastrophe on a par with the delivery failure of the Daily Mail or Daily Telegraph!

Mike's friend and side-kick in the apartments was a small man called Alan who tended to shake and stagger a bit due to Parkinson's Disease. He had been an administrator and although he had no financial involvement in any of Mike's businesses he was attracted to the thrill of the shady side, such a contrast from his many years as a conservative, respected Civil

Servant. Mike was glad to have Alan about because when things went wrong, or, when he overstepped the mark as frequently happened, it was good to have a companion like Alan to present a respectable acceptable face for the business.

Although as different as day is from night, the two men enjoyed each other's company and, like all old men, spent many happy hours repeating stories to each other totally unconcerned by the repetition.

Their repertoire had been replenished during the winter. It had been, just before Christmas, one of the coldest spells on record. The town lay under two to three feet of snow. Heavy snow even lay on the board walks of the Marina, which itself had frozen over, much to the surprise of the sea bird population.

Many roads were impassible and cars abandoned. In the local Casualty Department the tally of broken limbs, especially wrists, rose steadily.

In many ways however, the snow and the inconvenience caused by it, actually brought people together. Neighbours, who at best only nodded to each other, suddenly found a common purpose in helping to dig each others' cars out of the snowdrifts and conviviality spread through the district. In fact, it was a bit like the Dunkirk or Blitz spirit on a smaller scale.

The main thoroughfare passing the short roadway leading down to the apartments had not been treated or cleared by Roads Service. Hence it quickly became congested with abandoned cars. Mike and Alan decided to see what help they could be and, in doing so, had made numerous new acquaintances as they somewhat ineffectually spread sand and salt and pushed and dug to release stranded vehicles. Probably much more effective was the liberal communal use of Mike's large hip flask which required replenishment more frequently than the wheel barrow carrying the salt!

However the craic was good, stories were swapped and Mike and Alan, already well known by sight, became interesting and humourously rounded individuals in their neighbours' eyes. They enjoyed the interaction and missed the entertainment when the snow went and the population returned to work and their insular lives.

It would've been a good six weeks after the snow had vanished that the two friends were enjoying an Ulster fry for breakfast in a Main Street café and Alan was listening once again to Mike's description of how he had single-handedly prevented a skidding car from plunging down the steep slope and crashing into the children's playground. With each telling the danger to the children and the bravery of Mike became much greater.

"Wouldn't be surprised if they put up a statue to me", said Mike, "or maybe one of those blue plaques on the apartment wall".

"You usually have to be dead to get one of those" said Alan.

"But think of the lives I've saved".

Alan's attention, however, had been distracted by a very attractive young woman who passed by the café window on a number of occasions. Each time she hesitated as though she was going to enter but did not. Finally, she seemed to have picked up the courage and came through the door. Pausing for a moment to get her bearings, she then walked purposefully towards their table.

"May I join you?" she asked. Two male egos immediately replied "yes".

"My name is Claire Scott" she said "and I have a problem".

"Would you like to tell us how you feel about it ?" asked Alan who had been trained by the Samaritans. Claire gave him a strange look and directed her attention to Mike. "I've lost my sister" she said.

"Careless" was the response. "Would you like tea or coffee?"

"I'm serious" she said, then, as an afterthought, "Tea please, although it stains my teeth".

Alan was studying the woman. She was not as young as he had first thought. Her slim figure, long blonde hair and graceful movement gave the impression of youthful vitality. Her clothes were well cut and stylish, her shoes and handbag expensive, but what had captivated Alan were her startling blue eyes.

"Well you obviously know who we are" said Mike, "but what has the loss of your sister to do with us?"

"My sister has gone missing, I am at my wits' end and a mutual friend suggested that I speak to you".

"Why, what's it to us"?

"Well, she said you might know people, have contacts through your business interests that ordinary people would not have".

"Here, I hope I'm not getting a bad reputation. I'll have you know that my business interests are all completely legal and above board" said Mike. "You're not from the Inland Revenue are you?"

Alan looked again at the deep blue eyes which reflected trouble and sadness. "Maybe you should start at the beginning" he suggested.

Claire sipped her tea. "I am, sorry, I was a teacher. I've lived in this area for fifteen years. My husband is dead, I have two teenage sons and a sister. My parents are dead. My sister and I are closer now than we used to be, but we don't live in each other's pockets. She lives in Belfast. We ring each other a couple of times a week and meet up quite regularly. My problem is, for the last 4 weeks I have not been able to contact her".

"Have you done all the usual things, checked her house, spoken to neighbours, checked with her friends, told the police, spoken to her employer?" asked Alan.

"Of course I have" she snapped, "what do you take me for?"

"How about a neurotic, highly strung woman?" suggested Mike.

The blue eyes filled with tears. "I really am serious" she said.

"Could she have gone on holiday?" asked Alan.

No I don't think that is very likely and certainly she couldn't have gone far for I have the key to her house and when I checked it out, I saw that she had left her passport".

"I still don't see what we can do" said Mike.

"Perhaps if I explain a little more about my sister it would help. My sister and I were never alike. She was the wild one, expelled from 2 schools, ran away to London, a string of unsuitable, often criminal boyfriends, involvement in drugs and even at one stage, prostitution to fund her habit. Her activities I know shortened my parents' lives and they didn't know the half of it. They were so upset. I kept in touch with her but could not make her change. Then she met Tom who was to have a huge influence on her life. He had had his own drug issues to deal with when he was younger and was now acting as a part-time volunteer drug counsellor. By his willpower and influence over her, he managed to get her off drugs. She lived with him in London for five years and seemed happy and settled. However her happiness was cut short by 7/7 : the London bombings in July 2005. Tom was killed in one of the underground explosions. It was after that she decided to come back to Northern Ireland and she bought a house in Belfast. Although she has no qualifications, she is very clever and got a job working as a receptionist in a Doctor's surgery. Although she drank a fair amount, she did not, to the best of my knowledge, go back to drugs.

However, after Tom she never seemed to find anyone else to settle down with. I tried to introduce her to some friends but she didn't appear interested in any relationship. She seemed intent on keeping herself to herself. We talked, usually on the phone, at least once a week. About a couple of months ago I felt something had changed. I couldn't put my finger on it, but something was different. I tried to meet her for coffee a couple of times but she made excuses and for the past four weeks I have heard nothing"

As she talked Alan observed her closely. She was well spoken, highly articulate and obviously intelligent. Although upset, she remained calm and collected. However, he had the distinct impression that she was holding something back.

"I still don't see what this has to do with us" said Mike.

"I can find out nothing and no one I've spoken to, including the police, has been any help at all. Our mutual friend – who is Anne Ardis by the way, thought that through your activities you would have underworld contacts who might be helpful".

"God, you're making us sound like the Kray twins" said Mike, " and by the way, North Down doesn't have an underworld as such and if it did, it would need two, one for the Prods and one for the Taigs. I still don't see what we can do. This is a missing person enquiry. Sure there are over paid, under worked bodies that deal with things like this. Have you tried the welfare people or the Police? The Salvation Army might be able to help. After all, people go missing every day".

"I'm scared in case she has gone back to her old ways. I've a really bad feeling about it all". said Claire, her voice close to breaking.

Everyone fell silent. Alan was the first to speak.

"Perhaps we need to think for a moment what we're trying to say and do. Claire, you would like us to use whatever contacts Mike may have to find, or try to find, your sister? She, what's her name by the way?"

"Sarah" said Claire.

"Well, Sarah may well not want to be found".

"I feel so guilty", said Claire. "I don't think I looked after her well enough when she came back. I should have seen her more often, I should have asked her about the drugs. I should have talked more to her about Tom, I should have arranged to take her on holiday.

Really I've been a crap sister to her!"

"Claire" said Alan. "Don't beat yourself up over this. There are always plenty of people out there willing to do it for you, so don't lay the blame on yourself. You said Sarah wanted to keep herself to herself. You can't parachute into someone's life if they don't want you there. You're not responsible for her disappearance, no more than we can be made responsible for finding her".

Claire looked so dejected as she responded in a small voice. "Please help. No one else is interested. I thought even if you kept your ear to the ground, you might pick up a lead. "

"I don't think so" said Alan.

"Hold on" exclaimed Mike. "This might be interesting, something different, let's think about it for a couple of days. Leave your number Claire and we'll ring you.... Now back to the important things in life. I fancy another coffee and a German biscuit. I find a German biscuit always goes down well after an ulster fry!"

Claire stood up. "Thank you" she said. "My friend said I could trust you and that you wouldn't bullshit me. I look forward to hearing from you. "

With that she pulled her coat tighter around her, lifted her handbag and made her way to the door, Mike's eyes following every step.

"Mike, what are you doing?" asked Alan.

"Having a German biscuit. "

"Good job you haven't a sweet tooth" said Alan who was forever telling Mike off about his sugar consumption.

"Yes it is" replied Mike "because I notice they didn't bring me any marmalade for my fried bread this morning. "

"Seriously... what are you getting us into?" asked Alan.

"I don't really know but things have been getting a bit dull recently. This could be a golden opportunity. We could be a modern day Holmes and Watson".

"What made you think of that?"

"An old film I was watching the other afternoon. I quite fancied the pipe and hat!"

"Well" said Alan. "I'm not sure the Cohen brothers would see us as their first choice in the casting department".

"I think we're perfect for the roles".

"I hope you realise that Holmes came to a sticky end".

"Never knew it, what happened?"

"He's supposed to have had a fight with Professor Moriarty at the Reichenbach Falls in Switzerland, during which he fell to his death".

"OK. I'll not go near Switzerland, in fact I wont even go near the waterfall in the country park. Rest assured I will not place myself in any danger, you can sleep peacefully. Tomorrow I'll ask around and start talking to a few people to see what I can turn up".

"Do you really think something strange has happened to her sister?"

"I don't know, could be, or of course it could be just that I fancy Claire."

"What a surprise, so out of character!"

"I might know a man who could give us a steer although, to be honest, most of my friends would be dead pleased if the females closest to them vanished. They wouldn't spend time looking".

"You are such a romantic" said Alan. "Now let's test your memory. Whose turn is it to pay for breakfast?"

"Yours" came the immediate reply.

The two breakfast boys sauntered out of the café (if two old men could saunter!).

"What grade?" asked Mike.

"Maybe 6, no mushrooms and the tomato wasn't great" said Alan.

"I'm only going to give 5, the German biscuit was soggy".
"But it wasn't part of the breakfast, you can't score on it".
"O.K. I'll go to 5 ½."

They were on a mission to test and grade every breakfast provider in Bangor. Sort of Egon Ronay of the breakfast table, is how Alan described it.

On the walk back both men were pondering on the interview with Claire. Alan still felt she had been holding back on something, Mike hoped she wouldn't.

As they walked slowly up the hill towards the apartments Alan looked down to where the early spring sun was reflected in the calm water of the Marina. Some hardy souls were preparing their boats for the season. These were the ones which actually put to sea. Alan sometimes thought the others were only there for show, with no engines and plastic hulls made from Airfix kits!

The Marina was really quite large, catering not only to the local cohort of pleasure craft, but also to an increasing number of visitors, some from home waters, others from abroad, especially France and Germany and even, on occasions, yachts from Canada and the United States, putting in to replenish supplies.

Its construction had not been without controversy. It had meant the loss of the town beach and the creation of a huge area filled in to make a car park, which many considered an eyesore, but since the area facing the car park had never been redeveloped, and was now an even greater eyesore, the focus of blame had shifted to the Council. The Marina architects had done a thorough job, providing a new pier and harbour wall to protect the Marina, whilst also providing safe moorings for the large commercial craft and fishing boats. With an eye for detail, they had even provided nesting holes along the harbour walls for the resident guillemot population.

As they took the pedestrian path back towards their apartments, the wind started to rise, tugging at the rigging of the moored yachts. The musical sound created was like hearing hundreds of wind chimes and, coupled with the large number of palm trees and exotic shrubs that grew in the micro climate, the scene was more reminiscent of the Mediterranean than North Down.

"Why do you think Claire approached us" asked Mike, "I don't even know Ann Ardis all that well".

"I think, as she said, she's at her wits end and is clutching at straws. I also think that she has a problem with guilt but that it's misplaced. Sarah is responsible for her own actions. Besides, it looks as if the concern is largely on Claire's side. Sarah hasn't shown her much consideration in the past and even now you'd think she would contact her sister even just to say she was OK".

"Sometimes people behave strangely when they're under pressure" said Mike.

"Do you think she's in some sort of trouble, something serious?"

"I just don't know, but something isn't right. If I was Claire I too, would be worried", said Mike. "Still" he said with a smile and lightening his tone, "we'll do a bit of investigating and see what turns up and I think I'll get one of those deerstalker hats that Holmes wore. Do you think I'd look well in it?"

"You'll have to ask a deer!" said Alan.

CHAPTER 2

The next morning as Alan counted out his battery of pills to control the Parkinson's, he felt strangely elated. Life had been dull recently and when that was the case he tended to dwell pessimistically on the slow inexorable advance of the disease which had plagued him for 14 years. Maybe this would turn out to be a little adventure, at least for a time, which would give a sense of purpose to what had become recently a somewhat pointless existence.

He thought again about yesterday's meeting and his feeling that Claire still had more relevant information to divulge about her sister. He remembered the trouble and pain behind those blue eyes and suddenly realised they had expressed an element of fear as well.

Secretly he was quite taken with the idea of playing Watson to Mike's Holmes. As Watson had to cope with Holmes' heroin addiction, so too did he have to deal with Mike's binge drinking. Alan hoped that the little task in hand would steady Mike, who had been drinking more recently as his business interests declined. Just before 10.00 am the phone rang.

"Morning Watson" said the voice.

"Well, have you heard anything?"

"My contacts aren't up this early".

"Listen" said Mike "I've just realised we don't have Claire's sister's address. I think we should go to her place, get the address and key and go in to Belfast to see if we can turn anything up".

"O.K. " said Alan. "you ring and we will go about eleven. Now I am going to have my coffee before doing anything!".

Really, he thought to himself I am becoming a rigid, inflexible old man. Insisting on my coffee before I leave home! Next I will be refusing food other than at certain times. He remembered the father-in-law of a good friend who sulked if his tea was not on the table at five pm and shuddered at the thought of what he might become.

Next question to be considered was dress. A suit was easy and required little thought. Somehow with a suit, the choice of shirt and tie came naturally and there was no problem matching trousers.

Casual was very different and confusing. For a start there was the determination of style. What image was he trying to create? At his age what did image matter? Nonetheless he didn't want to appear foolish. Jeans he was never certain about, he had always associated them with youth but nearly everyone wore them. Then the issue of matching shirts, pullover if necessary and of course the jacket. Of course with the Parkinson's there was always the issue of doing up buttons which could sometimes take an age. Perhaps his clothes should be sorted and stored according to style and colour but really what a waste of time! He picked out a dark blue suit, white shirt and plain dark blue tie. To hell with fashion!

He made his way down to the underground garage where his old Mercedes sat. Although old it was in good order, as it should be considering the service bills he paid. He found it a comfortable car and since he had owned it for 20 years he knew its strengths and weaknesses well. Only rarely now did it do long journeys. He opened the car, got in and pressed the remote control for the garage door, which rolled up to reveal the neatly tended garden in which the residents took much pride, planting the borders and a selection of ceramic pots. In the summer it was a riot of colour. A large wooden table and benches provided a summer focus for communal BBQs which helped cement good community relations and to which everyone contributed food and, more importantly, drink!

Mike was sitting over at the table and as the car emerged from the garage he stood up expectantly. His dress was to say the least - striking!. He was wearing a Bavarian/Tyrolean jacket of a style last seen in Berchtesgaden in 1938, stained white trousers, denim shirt with Donald Duck motif, Doc Martin boots, baseball cap and sunglasses!

"Well" said Alan "no one is going to miss you in that outfit".

"I think I look well" replied Mike, "I have the height to carry it off".

"Height of nonsense more like, now shut up and get in "

Claire lived in a substantial detached house off what was called Bangor's Ring Road, easy to get to but really the house could have been in a suburban development anywhere. Not even within easy walking distance of the town centre or coastal path, the only claim the house had to justify the estate agent's description "appealing location", was that it was next door to a huge shopping centre. However, it suited Claire and she had never seriously considered moving.

As Alan and Mike drew up outside, Claire stepped out from the front door, walked down the short driveway and gave a key to Mike.

"I have to go out" she said, "you know where Sarah's house is, didn't I give you the address over the phone?"

"That your car?" asked Alan looking at a black Golf GTI parked in the driveway.

"One of my little weaknesses" admitted Claire, "I have always had a thing for cars".

"Funny I never put her down as a petrol head" said Alan as they swung onto the dual carriageway to Belfast. Within two miles they were reduced to walking pace.

"Bloody road works" said Mike, "they must have more cones for use on this road than in the rest of the country. Are you sure they aren't running a degree course in the Tech on Cone Placing and using this road for practicals!"

It took them over an hour to get to Belfast.

The house, in which Claire's sister Sarah lived, was a small townhouse in a quiet, residential area near the Museum. The area, part of the University district, was a great favourite with students and academics which gave it a liberal bohemian air. The housing was mixed. Large three storied Victorian houses rubbed shoulders with good quality terrace housing which, in some cases, had been cleared to build new townhouses. It was in one of these that Sarah lived.

She had always liked the area, the proximity to the University, the Botanical Gardens, the Museum, the rebuilt Lyric Theatre (the newest theatre in Belfast) and the village style shopping area of Stranmillis held a great appeal for someone whose lifestyle had been, for want of a better term, described as "alternative".

When she returned to Belfast she immediately contacted a local Estate Agent and to her great delight, discovered that a new townhouse in the area had just come on the market. Ideally she would have preferred an older property, perhaps one which looked out over Botanic Gardens with its wonderful Palm House and Tropical Ravine, but no such property was for sale and even if it had been, her budget would never have stretched to it.

Her house was easy to pick out due to its bright yellow door to the left of which was a colourful flower arrangement in a hanging basket.

Feeling self-conscious they walked up the narrow path to the front door and inserted the Chubb key into the good quality seven lever dead lock. "At least Sarah took security seriously" thought Alan.

Stepping through the doorway, stopping to pick up the post, they found themselves in an open plan ground floor area. Alan looked around. The house had a bright airy feel, the fabrics both in curtains and furniture were lightly coloured, giving the impression of brightness and space and the natural wood flooring had been sanded down and finished to a very high standard. Two large abstract paintings dominated wall space. Furniture was limited to a settee and two single chairs with a couple of vases and an occasional table with an attractive lamp sitting on it. Obviously Sarah believed William Morris when he said that nothing should be in a home that was not either useful or beautiful. The kitchen looked as if it was seldom used. Sarah obviously did not do much entertaining.

Everything seemed normal. Perhaps too normal, thought Alan. He couldn't imagine a woman going away, leaving tights, leggings and a sweater over the back of a dining room chair or the remains of fresh food in the fridge.

Mike in the meantime had gone upstairs. "Watson" he called down, "she's left her contraceptive pills in the bathroom cabinet, she must be away on a religious retreat".

"You shouldn't be going through her things – give her some privacy".

"But how can we find her if we haven't got clues to go on? Sherlock Holmes by this time would have worked out her age, weight, eye colour, preferred method of travel, date and time of departure and destination, plus her financial position".

"Well you are not Holmes" muttered Alan.

"No" said Mike "but I have got the answers. Age we know, height and eye colour from her passport which I have in front of me, financial position from her bank balance which is also here, plus a train timetable with some of the Enterprise services to Dublin underlined. So my dear Watson, our missing person has gone to Dublin on a religious retreat. Case solved!"

Alan unlocked the back door and stepped out into a small flagged rear yard, festooned with colourful flower pots and separated from the house next door by a wood panel fence.

"You here about the house?" a voice said.

Alan turned around to see a tall, plumpish, red haired, young woman peering over the fence.

"Er – yes" he replied defensively.

"You married?" she continued, then Mike strode into view.

"This your partner?" she asked looking him up and down. "Don't worry, people round here are very liberal, as long as you're not a Paedo" she added.

"I certainly am not either, a partner or a Paedo", blustered Mike beginning to wonder if the white trousers had been such a good idea, never mind the Bavarian jacket!

"Anyway what's this about the house?" Mike asked the woman.

"The other two men who were here just a couple of days ago said the house was being put up for sale, so I naturally thought you might be potential new neighbours".

"We're just looking on behalf of a friend, getting a feel for the place" said Alan.

"Oh it's a lovely neighbourhood, my name is Lily by the way".

"This is Mike and I am Alan. Do you know the woman who lives here?"

"Not very well, would you like a wee cup of tea?"

"No thanks" said Alan.

"Not even a wee cup in your hand" persuaded Lily in her best hospitable Belfast manner. "It's easier to talk over a cup of tea".

"Alright, you have persuaded us" said Mike.

"Come round the front" said Lily, "it's nice that people are friendly, those other two were very stuck up, you could get nothing out of them. "

Although the two houses were structurally identical, Lily's house was as different from Sarah's as day is from night! Where Sarah's house breathed light and openness, Lily's lounge was dark and oppressive. Dark venetian blinds coupled with dark curtains, carpets and furniture gave it an almost funereal feel. On one wall was a picture of a tiger, on the other, three flying ceramic ducks. A sideboard and table were covered with a variety of cheap ornaments. No books were obvious and one corner was dominated by a huge television. The house lacked a feminine touch – but then Lily did not appear to be very feminine. The wall of the entrance hall was covered with photographs of football teams and players!

Seated in Lily's lounge in a less than comfortable chair, a cup and saucer sitting precariously on a none too steady knee, Alan began to enquire about Sarah.

"Oh she was popular enough but kept herself to herself, seldom had visitors although the occasional man called. I think it was all above board not that it mattered anyway with her being single and all. We certainly never heard anything not even with the glass against the wall. She is a good looking woman, some of the local men had an eye for her but she never gave any encouragement – the ice maiden, they nicknamed her. She works in the Doctor's surgery beside the castle but according to my cousin she hasn't been at work for weeks. I was thinking that maybe she had to go back to London where she used to live".

Mike who was studying a photograph on the small table,"Is that your husband Dessi Platt who plays for the Swifts?"

"Yes but he is no longer a full time professional. Now he plays part time and drives a taxi".

"A fine player. You must be proud of him". Lily said nothing.

"Who were the two men who were here a few days ago?" asked Alan.

"I thought they were Estate Agents although now I remember it, my husband thought one was a policeman but I suppose with so many police being made redundant it's possible he could have started a second career. In a way, being in the police is good training for an estate agent since they both have an elastic view of the truth".

"You can say that again" said Mike with feeling.

"Has she any special friends?" asked Alan.

"Not really, she had a sister and another girl used to call sometimes".

"It's very kind of you to give us tea" said Mike "we have taken up enough of your time. We'll be able to tell our friend how welcoming and nice the neighbours are".

"I always say it's nice to be nice" said Lily getting to her feet. "Has your friend made an offer and do you know what it is?"

"It's not quite at that stage yet" said Mike.

Lily looked disappointed.

In the car Alan turned to Mike. "What was the rush? I had more questions to ask".

"That's what I was scared of. You were like a fucking policeman with all those questions. We may think Sarah's missing but no one else knows anything. We might be barking up the wrong tree, and so many questions from an odd couple looking over a property for a friend is bound to raise suspicion".

"Inspector Rebus would have asked" Alan said.

"You think you are a fucking detective now, why don't you get a flashing blue light for the top of your car?" Mike slumped down in his seat.

"It's a good job I don't take offence easily" said Alan, but nonetheless a stoney silence fell across the car. Alan turned on Radio 3 to fill the vacuum.

Thirty minutes later they were outside Claire's house, road cones en route having been removed.

"There doesn't appear to be anyone here" said Mike, "I'll drop the key through the letterbox".

On his way back from the door he was accosted by a young spiderman on what appeared to be a very fancy bike which was at least two sizes too big for him.

"She's not in" said the child.

"I know, I'm not stupid" said Mike looking balefully at his would be interrogator.

"The other men didn't get her either" said the child knowingly.

"Who were they?" asked Mike falling into the trap.

"Dunno but their car was better than yours"

"Why was that my little spider?"

"It was armoured" said the boy proudly.

"How do you know?"

"Obvious innit?" "Is that jacket fancy dress?"

"Spiders lead very dangerous lives" said Mike "take care you are not trodden on my little friend".

"Did you hear that?" said Mike on his return to the car.

"Yes" responded Alan, "I thought Spiderman won on points".

"Very funny. Do you think that the two men here are the same two who visited Sarah's pretending to be Estate Agents, although we only have Lily's opinion on that. I wonder did she see their car?"

"I told you we needed to ask more questions".

Alan was ignored.

"If the car was armoured it was certainly police" said Mike "but usually missing persons' enquiries are carried out by uniform branch. I really don't understand why the hell detectives would be involved. When we get back I'll start to make some enquiries.

There is certainly something strange going on".

"We need to talk to Claire again" said Alan. "There's something we are not being told. Give her a ring and say we need to meet. In the meantime we need to consider our position and just what we're getting into".

"I wonder if Sarah is as good looking as Claire" mused Mike "This family is starting to interest me".

They drove back slowly through the teatime Bangor traffic. Turning into the narrow lane leading to the apartment, Alan let the heavy Mercedes coast down the steep slope, stopping at the bottom to wait for the automatic bollard to respond to the remote control and slip into the ground to let them pass.

As he reversed the car into the underground garage Alan remarked, "This always reminds me of the Batmobile being parked in the Bat Cave".

"Can I be Batman?" enquired Mike. "You can be Robin!"

"Do you not think we have enough on our plates with Holmes and Watson to look after? Besides we are getting too old for this. "

"Nonsense Watson, we are in our prime, besides, what harm can we do?"

Famous last words .... or they nearly were!

CHAPTER 3

The armoured Vauxhall Omega crunched on its suspension stops as it was driven rapidly over the speed ramp.

"What's the rush?" said Derek Linton, an Inspector in the Counter Terrorist Command.

"Don't like this area" said Sergeant Clive Smyth. "Has bad memories for me and this car sticks out like a sore thumb. Why are we in it anyway?"

"Only cars left in the pool this morning were armoured ones. No one wants them anymore, they are only needed in South Armagh and Lurgan. "

"Should have given South Armagh to the South years ago. Why are we looking for this woman anyway, sure it's something the uniforms would normally do and why the great secrecy?"

"Apparently she absconded with some government equipment" said Linton.

"What? All this over a bloody typewriter".

"Don't do typewriters any longer".

"Well alright – a computer then, sure you can buy them for three hundred quid".

"Ours not to reason why, only ours to do and die".

"I'm not in the mood for quotations but I am in the mood for a Big Mac. Let's pull into the McDonalds beside the hospital".

"Neat location, so convenient for the heart patients" commented Linton.

Sergeant Smyth ignored the snide comment. He and Derek

Linton had worked together for years, although not always as partners. They knew each other well, recognised and ignored each other's little foibles and eccentricities because they recognised the complete trust each had in the other.

They had served together during some of the worst times of the Troubles, had sympathised and supported each other through their divorces and shared the problems posed by growing adolescent families.

They lived quite close to each other and had socialised together as families before their marriages had broken down. Now their socialisation consisted of a few beers in a local bar considered safe for use by security personnel.

Something else linked them. In the early days of the troubles, Clive Smyth had, by his quick thinking, saved Derek Linton's life, in fact he'd saved both their lives.

They'd been on patrol along the border when they came across an abandoned car. Linton, then a Sergeant, cautiously left the patrol car and had walked gingerly over to the abandoned vehicle. Smyth, meanwhile, had left the driver's seat and walked over to the side of the road. Then he saw it, the black command wire running into a culvert just beneath where Linton was standing. Shouting a warning to Linton he bent down and cut the wire. Both men dived back into the police car as the gunfire broke out from the hillside on the other side of the border.

Smyth threw the car into reverse and, with tyres screeching, executed a 180 degree turn. Foot hard down on the accelerator he zig zagged up the road and out of the ambush.

Although the car was hit several times both officers escaped injury.

"How does the Boss expect us to find this woman when we're not allowed to ask questions or even admit she's missing and will her sister not think that we're now overreacting to her plea for help? People can feel these things".

"I told you, we explain to the sister that we're part of a new team tasked with increasing the identification rate of missing persons".

"I didn't like that nosey neighbour, far too much to say for herself. Besides an Estate Agent should know about house prices etc. We didn't come over as very believable Estate Agents".

"It was the first thing came into my head to explain why we were in the house without raising concern. We didn't find anything anyway".

"It would have been easier if we knew what we were looking for".

"I keep telling you, we were just there to check if she had left voluntarily or if there was any indication she was abducted. Everything seemed normal".

"I note she hadn't taken her rabbit with her".

"I saw no rabbit, if someone is feeding it they might know where she has gone to".

"This rabbit lives in her knicker drawer!".

"You sick old man, what were you doing in her knicker drawer anyway?".

"Just looking for what we don't know".

"For the last time we're not looking for anything, we're simply trying to determine if she left voluntarily".

"So you say".

"The car will stink after the burger".

"Maybe I should eat in the car park, if you're going to be so fussy!"

Silence descended as they bit to their Big Macs with fries and coke.

"Must drop into the police gym someday" said Sergeant Smyth.

CHAPTER 4

"Watson" said the voice at the end of the line.

"Mike, not normal for you to be up so early, it's just after eight".

"Up early, I haven't been to bed yet. I told you my contacts are all night birds, creatures of the darkness, children of the "shadows". "

"Very poetical, have you been drinking?"

"Only a little, I thought you liked poetry – there's a green eyed yellow idol to the north of Katmandu, would you like me to sing the "Aul Orange Flute"?"

"Never mind all of that, I take it since you're ringing at this time you've discovered something?"

"Not a lot, but there is a lot of activity. It seems that the government has lost something and is taking steps to get it back. Mind you they seem to be running about like headless chickens with their heads stuffed up their arses".

"Mixed metaphor, Holmes".

"I wouldn't know one if it bit my arse".

"What else have you found out?"

"Nothing really, it's times like this that the ODCs (ordinary decent criminals) hate. It is so disruptive to business to have all this activity. You never know what they might find. Bad for business, no one even knows what's missing".

"Do you think it has anything to do with our missing Sarah?"

"I think it is probably just a coincidence".

"It's time to talk with Claire again, give her a ring after breakfast".

"Who's in charge here Watson?"

"My dear Holmes, who has the car?"

"Point taken. We'll go about ten – if that's alright?"

"Sounds good" said Alan as he hung up and took a violent stagger to his left. Must try not to do that in public he thought. At least the disease hadn't affected his brain in the intellectual sense and for that he was thankful. It could be a few more years before he would need either a late night swim or a one way ticket to Switzerland.

He turned his mind back to the case as he now considered it. If they could find the female visitor, she might give a clue.

The old Mercedes climbed up the steep hill from the apartments with Bangor's Holmes and Watson on board.

"Pity you lost your license" said Alan "I don't always feel like driving".

"Sure we could always take a taxi" said Mike "there's always plenty of them about".

"Not when you need one!"

"I see, it's going to be one of those days".

Their bickering ceased as they threaded their way down the narrow, traffic infested Dufferin Avenue, commonly called Suffering Avenue due to the large number of flats occupied by DHSS clients and also because it was the address of the Bangor branch of the Samaritans.

"You know" said Alan "tracking our missing person is probably a violation of their human rights so if we find Sarah she could probably sue us!"

"I wouldn't worry too much" said Mike "with our lack of experience and expertise the chances of success aren't great and remember, I only agreed to look into it in the hope of getting at look at something else, if you know what I mean".

The Regent Hotel was one of the oldest in the area. An old Victorian structure, it had provided genteel accommodation for holiday makers for decades. Now, however, holiday makers would not thank you for a week in Bangor; the Costas were too cheap and inviting, so the hotel catered mainly now for commercial customers plus short weekend breaks, heavily advertised in Scotland, the shortest and cheapest Irish Sea Ferry crossing to Larne being a big attraction to the Scots.

Inside, the hotel still boasted dark wooden panelling in its public rooms and a dining room with panoramic views to die for over Bangor, the view hopefully distracting the diners' attention from the seriously worn carpet at their feet. Decayed splendour would perhaps best describe the establishment and the elderly clients who still frequented it.

They had arranged to meet Claire in the ground floor coffee dock of the hotel, where the service was poor, the coffee virtually undrinkable but, not surprisingly, there were very few other customers to eavesdrop on conversations.

"She's late" grumbled Mike.

"Well we didn't give her very much notice" said Alan.

"Don't like being kept waiting by a woman, disturbs the natural balance of life".

"Are you always so closely in touch with your feminine side?" said Alan, getting to his feet to welcome Claire.

"Sorry I'm late, parking you know".

"No odds" said Mike," We were just discussing some of the deeper philosophical issues of life".

"We haven't really made much headway" Alan said, "We were wondering if you could throw some more light on the subject, for example, who might visit your sister and why she was putting the house up for sale?"

Bewilderment flashed across Claire's face.

"I don't understand" she said "My sister wasn't planning to sell. What makes you think she was?"

Mike looked at her. "She had a couple of Estate Agents visit the property".

"I'm astonished".

"Have the police been in touch with you?"

"Funny you should ask, but I got a note pushed through the letterbox from something called the Identification of Missing Persons Branch saying they wished to talk to me".

"Never heard of IMPB" said Mike "and I've had contact with most branches. Still, this new post-Patton police force has its own strange ways of going about things. Anyway let's get back to your sister. None of my contacts seem to know anything but then why should they? After all they do walk on different sides of the street".

"I brought this photograph of Sarah, I thought it might be helpful.

Alan looked at the photograph. Sarah was shorter and heavier than Claire with dark hair but they shared the same handsome features and, as far as Alan could tell the same deep blue eyes. Although she was not smiling in the photograph, Alan could detect that electric vitality which must be generic to the family.

"We could turn it into a missing person's poster" suggested Mike.

"No!" came the instant response. "I don't want the whole thing publicised".

She squirmed in her seat looking distinctively uncomfortable.

Alan leaned across the table.

"Why do I think you are holding something back?"

Claire pulled her cashmere coat more tightly around her and lifted her handbag as if preparing to depart. Then she appeared to have second thoughts, sat back and relaxed.

"Let me go back and fill in some details" she said.

"I told you Sarah had a really bad time in London before she was rescued by Tom. What I didn't say was that Tom worked undercover for the Anti Terrorist Squad and what I didn't know until after his death, was that he had got approval from his superiors and inducted Sarah into the same organisation. She was working alongside him, infiltrating organisations, collecting information, bugging telephones, shadowing suspects. In fact Tom was on the underground that day because he was tailing one of the bombers. I only found this out by chance a good bit later. I was at a function for the relatives of those killed on 7/7 where the drink was flowing freely. Trying to charm his way into my pants, this rather handsome young intelligence officer revealed in more ways than one, more than he should have. However, all told it was a very pleasant night but one which left me with more questions than answers. I did try to speak to Sarah about it but she clammed up and became very agitated and defensive".

"What about the pillow talk boyfriend?" asked Mike "could he not give more details?"

"Oh that was only a one night stand, I don't even know his name". Mike's eyes lit up!

"What I'm beginning to think" she continued "is that she remained in touch with the anti-terrorist branch when she came back to Northern Ireland, maybe even working for them".

"But of course you never asked her" said Alan.

"I know, I know. I was just so relieved that she had settled after Tom's death and I didn't want to endanger our new close, but still fragile, relationship",

"What about her friends" asked Mike "would they know anything?"

"She really had no close friends, no one ever visited her".

"Not what the neighbour says. She claims men sometimes visited and in particular there was one woman whom she saw quite regularly".

"Maybe work mates" said Claire "she certainly never mentioned anyone to me".

"Where do we go from here?" asked Alan.

"I need a drink" said Mike, "how about you Claire?"

"Bit early for me but could we have some lunch?"

The trio left the Regent Hotel and walked the short distance to the Northern Bistro – 'Half Price for Pensioners' said the sign outside. Mike was caught in a dilemma. On the one hand he did not want to admit his age to Claire, but on the other hand he did not want to pay the full price for the meal! He compromised. Speaking to Claire in an undertone he said,

"They usually let me have the pensioner's rate when I come in with Alan, they say it's actually easier for them to calculate the bill"

Claire smiled, "only a man" she thought.

"What did your husband do?" enquired Alan as he picked up a menu.

"He was a chef, died in a motorbike accident".

"I'm sorry to hear that" said Alan, "what happened?"

"Must be nearly twelve years ago now. He was mad about motorbikes, the bigger the better. His pride and joy was a vintage Harley Davidson which he was always working on, but he also had a Kawasaki 750cc which he used to go back and forwards to the restaurant in the Castlereagh hills where he worked. He was a skilful, careful rider, but late one night, coming home after work, he hit a patch of ice and careered into some ranch fencing which had the planks on the outside of the posts rather than where they should be, on the inside, so that they can spring off harmlessly. As it was, one of the bars broke and went through his chest like a lance. Death must have been immediate, at least that's what I tell myself because it was daylight before anyone noticed the accident.

"I assumed he was staying in the restaurant which he sometimes did if he was really late or the weather was bad. You can imagine the shock it was to me when two police constables, a man and a woman, came to the door with the news at breakfast time, just as I was getting the children ready for school. It took me ages to recover, but life had to go on for the sake of the children, if nothing else. "

"Ever think of re-marrying?" enquired Mike.

"No, what about you?"

"Married and divorced three times. A Swede, a German and an Irish girl... Plus a few more relationships on the way".

"Still living in hope" said Alan, somewhat sourly.

"A pity I'm too young for you" said Claire playfully, much to Alan's amusement.

Mike said nothing.

"I don't want to be negative" said Alan, "but we are not really getting very far".

"Oh I don't mind" said Mike, "I'm getting to know Claire much better".

"Hardly the point of the exercise" murmured Claire.

"Right" said Alan, "let's look at what we know. She left voluntarily, albeit in a bit of a rush. She left her passport behind so she wasn't intending to go abroad".

"Shit... I've just remembered, she also had an Irish passport", said Claire.

"So she could be soaking up the sun in Spain".

"... Doesn't like the sun".

"How do we think she left Belfast – plane, car, train, bus or taxi".

"We'll have to check them all out" said Mike "We need to go round with her photograph and see if anyone remembers her. We'll start with the car hire people, then the bus and train staff".

"What we need is a lucky break". said Alan, "Remember" he added, "if it should be the police she's running from, she'll not want to use her passport because she could be picked up on computer too easily. Same for hire car, she would've needed to give her licence details".

"She cleared her current account, about £700 in it. Not a fortune. We can assume she didn't lease a luxury yacht from the Marina. That leaves bus or train. We really need a lucky break".

Which were exactly the same words Commander Harris was using in the King's Military Complex just about 9 miles away.

"Will both gentlemen be having the Pensioner's lunch as usual?" enquired the waiter.

CHAPTER 5

For Sarah everything had been fine until about a couple of months ago. That was when the approach had been made. At first she thought the dark handsome stranger with his dog was just being friendly, then she became concerned that he was trying to chat her up, but finally with gut wrenching fear she realised the truth.

In London, when she'd been working undercover with Tom, she'd been a guinea pig for a new eavesdropping approach. Perhaps because she'd led such a chaotic life, or perhaps because they thought that after all the injections and cuts she'd inflicted upon herself, a few more minor operations would not matter. They performed a breast enhancement. In one of the silicone sacs was a little speech capturing device linked wirelessly to what appeared to be a small mole on her lower neck but was actually a very powerful minute microphone. Finally, just at the base of her left thumb an incision was made and an on/off switch and battery inserted beneath the skin. She didn't need to be wired with a listening device for her undercover activities – she was the device.

However, Tom had died before much use could be made of it, and she'd sought sympathy from her superiors and received their blessing to opt out for a time and return to Belfast. For nearly four years she'd lived in what she now realised was a fool's paradise, believing that all had been forgotten about, that her spying days were over, that no longer would she have to try to infiltrate groups whose very smell she hated. Groups she was expected to join, support, even fuck, if necessary to gather intelligence about their plans, personnel and activities.

She suddenly became conscious again of the man standing beside her.

"We never really had the chance to test your new equipment" he said, eyeing her breasts.

"I've finished with all that" said Sarah, "when Tom died I said I wanted out. They agreed, they said it was O. K. ".

"You don't want to believe everything you're told. You've been on a little break and now you have a few tasks to perform".

"I'm not doing anything" she said "I don't work for you any longer".

"My dear, what a short memory. Remember the small matter of five unspent drug convictions".

"So what, put me in jail, I've been there before, it's not too bad".

"I guarantee this time will be much worse, but that's not significant. Now what would be really sad would be if you were to introduce those two young men, your sister's boys, to heroin and see them hooked".

"Not possible, they would never touch drugs".

"No, but we can arrange for the drugs to touch them. We arrange a week when they are supposed to be with you and I guarantee the treatment we administer will have them heroin addicts before the week is up. All your fault, a return to your old ways... dear, dear, what a shame".

She was at a loss for words.

"Bye, we'll be in touch in the near future. Enjoy your walk".

Frank Burns had been a MI5 operative for nearly 15 years. Recruited straight from University, he found that he greatly enjoyed the type of work he was asked to do, much of it in isolation, which as an only child he was well used to anyway. He had seen service in the Middle East, Afghanistan and Kosovo and was now operating as a liaison officer with the PSNI. He was popular with his colleagues and well thought of by his superiors but he was not a happy man.

For one thing he did not enjoy his liaison work with PSNI. They just didn't co-operate easily, and at his level he did not get on with his main contact in PSNI, there was a distinct personality clash.

Maybe more importantly he felt he had mishandled his latest task. It should have been straightforward to reactivate a dormant agent. Usually such people have been enthusiastic about returning to service but, if not, gentle pressure usually worked. Never before had he doubted the steps taken to achieve desired results. He considered himself a cold untouchable individual for whom the task in hand was everything. He was good at getting results because he was dispassionate and a good judge of where an individual's areas of weakness lay.

However, with Sarah he knew he had gone over the top. There had been no need for the threats against Claire's sons. It was almost as if he was trying to impress her with his power. He felt he had a lot of issues to resolve, but was not yet prepared to begin the investigation.

Back at home Sarah reviewed her position. The more she thought about it the more she realised she had to flee or else disclose everything. But to whom could she disclose? Who could be trusted? She thought briefly about Wikileaks but dismissed the idea. To disclose, she knew, would jeopardise ongoing operations, maybe put lives at risk and most certainly make her an expendable item.

Flight then was the answer. Away to a safe haven for a period of time, perhaps then everyone could come to their senses and some sort of honourable discharge could be arranged.

But where to go? She had both a British and Irish passport but decided not to head abroad since she could so easily be picked up at the airport. Instead she cleared her current account, packed a small rucksack with essentials and dressed in outdoor hiking gear, caught a bus to central station where she boarded the train to Derry, intending from there to hide out somewhere in Donegal.

She sat back in the carriage feeling more relaxed and took the opportunity to marvel at the scenery between Coleraine and Derry. The ruins of Downhill Castle; the Mussenden Temple, which was, she remembered, a library for the eccentric 18th century Earl Bishop of Derry, perched impossibly close to the edge of the cliff, the tunnel punched through the rocks beneath the Temple; the steep cliffs to the left beloved by gliding enthusiasts and to her right the beautiful and deserted Benone strand stretching for miles.

On arrival in Derry, she took the shuttle bus from the station to the city bus depot and joined a queue boarding the Letterkenny Express. She had spoken to no-one and had paid for everything in cash.

She spent the night in a rundown B&B on the Port Road giving her name as Brigid McDonald. She slept well.

The next morning, avoiding conversation with the landlady, she took a tip from the Dice-Man and threw an imaginary dice to correspond to the grid sections on her Donegal Activity Map. Viewing the outcome, she was less than pleased for the area identified was Sand Head, a small promontory with only single track access. The nearest village was Duncarry.

She headed down to Letterkenny bus station looking at the shops as she passed. She would have liked to spend an hour or two browsing in them, but she knew the longer she spent in any busy commercialised area, the greater the danger of being recognised or at least noticed. She had been aware of the cameras at the railway stations but saw no cameras covering the departure area. She moved quickly across, looking for a bus to Duncarry but saw no sign. She had just assumed there would be a bus, but perhaps there wasn't. She saw no option but to ask someone, although she desperately didn't want to draw any attention to herself. She looked around and decided to ask a teenage youth carrying a skateboard, in the belief that if anyone was to question him in the future, he would have much more on his mind than a middle-aged woman asking about a bus.

"The Swilly Bus Company don't run that route any longer" he said, answering her question. "You need to get one of the private coaches. There's an O'Donnell Coach at about eleven this morning. You get it from the other side of the roundabout at the end of Port Road".

Sarah thanked him and decided to head back into the town to put in the hour and a half she had to wait. Deciding on a cup of coffee, she chose a busy establishment where a woman on her own would not be noticed. Before she entered she bought a local paper and then, perched on a high stool at a round high table, she sipped her latte and opened her paper. She quickly realised the folly of buying a local paper since it dealt with local issues about which she knew nothing. She was sure it was important that the Garda Siochana supervised the sheep dipping, and looked with some interest at what was on in the cinema, but could not generate any interest in the parochial notes of the local chapels or the coffee morning of the Church of Ireland. The Gaelic football pages were passed as were the pages of car advertisements. In fact, she thought, a waste of money. There was some space given to the rise of dissident activity in the North. How, she wondered after all Ireland approval of the Good Friday Agreement, could a group of political and social misfits hope to justify their use of violence? Who did they represent? What did they hope to achieve by violence that could not be better done through democratic politics?.

Leaving the paper behind, she made her way to the roundabout. A coach carrying the name O'Donnell sat by the kerb, half full, but without a driver. Shortly a young man climbed into the drivers' seat, looked around and asked, "Are we missing anyone".

"Mary McAfee said to wait for her, she wont be long. She was getting a perm", said an elderly lady sitting in the third row of seats.

Sarah went up to the driver. "I want to go to Duncarry" she said.

"You're in luck, so do I" said the young man taking the money she offered but producing no ticket.

"Do I not need a ticket?". She asked

"Why" he said "sure you have paid".

Accepting the logic, she returned to her seat.

After about ten minutes Mrs McAfee turned up, her head a mass of tight blue curls. "Thanks for waiting Vincent" she said.

"Sure we couldn't go without you Mrs McAfee - your uncle owns the bus".

Thankful to have a seat to herself, Sarah gazed at the ever changing scenery, mountains, lakes, tidal inlets, small villages, stone walls, castles, sandy beaches, "It really is a most beautiful part of the world" thought Sarah. Stick a Disney sign on the gate and you have a theme park. In fact the whole country, North and South could be signed over to the Disney Corporation who would make a much better job of running it than the present politicians.

Passing an old deserted derelict ballroom in the middle of nowhere, she was reminded of William Trevor's short story

"The Ballroom of Romance", and was glad she had downloaded his short stories on to her Kindle. What could be better reading material for a stay in Donegal?

Duncarry, which they reached after about 40 minutes and a few stops, was very much a one street village, which, true to perverse Irish tradition, had turned its backside to its most scenic feature, in this case the sea and a long view down a deep sea lough to the Atlantic. Visitors to the village could well never have realised its coastal position unless they had driven, or walked about a mile southwards, to its small harbour overlooked by a gift shop and coffee house.

At the North end of the village stood what had once been a popular progressive hotel, now sadly fallen on hard times, its swimming pool leaking, the wooden floor of its squash court warping and its tennis court overgrown. It still attracted however a loyal following, mostly elderly guests for whom the peace of the village, the good, if traditional food and the warm welcome were the main attractions.

On the hills behind the village, the years of the Celtic Tiger economy had seen extensive development, mostly holiday homes for Dubliners and Northerners. This influx of holidaymakers had changed the nature of Duncarry. A new and very up to date supermarket had opened, its shelves stocked with items locals in the past would never have asked for, although it must be said they were now becoming more adventurous in their eating habits. Two speciality restaurants opened between Easter and Halloween, with tables at weekends requiring advance booking. A modern filling station had replaced an old ramshackle garage and beside it was a modern repair centre for cars and boats.

The two traditional pubs in the village hadn't changed at all, that was their charm. During the season they boasted live music with Irish folk groups in attendance.

The road out to the harbour passed the Garda station which provided both a police function and accommodation for the Sergeant and his family, and the Chapel. A very fine Chapel, of which the community was justifiably proud and where Mass was still well attended.

The harbour, with its 19th century pier, was not now used for commercial purposes, but rather as a summer mooring for pleasure craft, and as a picturesque place for tourists to visit or use as the starting point for walks into the hills.

Sarah decided to buy essentials from the supermarket, hoping she would be able to rent a caravan out at Sandhead. Her activity map indicated a number of caravan parks. It was about five miles out to Sandhead and with no bus service, she had no option but to walk. Still, it was a fine day, so, tightening the laces on her boots, she set off.

The road climbed steeply alongside a golf course which obviously belonged to the large hotel down by the beach. A multitude of electric golf carts stood by the door. Obviously the pampered guests had no intention of doing much walking even in pursuit of their sport. At the top of the hill she looked back at the beautiful white sands of a curving beach which must have stretched for miles. To her right was a sign for Mary's Bay where a number of fishing boats were moored. She continued her journey with the hills to her left and sea to her right. About half way to Sand Head, she came across an old graveyard resting in a hollow between the road and the sea. It appeared to have been an early monastic settlement. The early Christian monks certainly could pick a site and appreciated the importance of location, she thought.

Sarah sat on top of a smooth tombstone feeling the surprisingly strong early spring sun on her back, listening to the cry of the gulls and the bark of the seals from the rocks below. She looked idly at the gravestones, many dating back to the 1700s, and unmarked ones she was sure pre-dating those by hundreds of years. The same names appearing year after year, attested to a now largely vanished social permanence.

About a mile further along, Sarah decided on a little detour and, after checking her map, left the road and headed across the common land. In places it was very marshy, and as she felt dampness invade her boots, she began to wonder just how good an idea it was. One of the reasons for the detour was to see the large rock cross erected at the foot of a small hill with a smooth rock table beneath. It had been the gift of an American philanthropist who reckoned that the people of the peninsula should have somewhere to hear Mass to save them going to Duncarry Chapel. However, the local populace and Sarah could agree with them on this, preferred the walk to a comfortable Chapel to hear Mass, rather than standing often in the rain, on sodden, marshy ground.

Leaving the site of the rock altar, she made her way to a jewel of a beach facing the Atlantic with huge breakers rolling in. She was sure it must be a paradise for surfers in summer. At the end of the beach, which was strewn with all sorts of interesting debris, much of it from Canada and the USA, was a small mountain which she had decided to climb.

It was an easy climb, following sheep tracks to near the summit. The view was magnificent, a panorama of sea, mountains and beaches. Of particular attraction to her was a small bay beneath where she was standing. It was a very steep slope leading down to it, but she reckoned she could make it in safety.

On the beach she noted how dangerous the waves appeared to be, breaking on offshore rocks and swirling into the beach, creating rip currents which would have been very difficult to swim against. At one end of the beach was a cave just waiting to be explored, which she had no hesitation in doing, marvelling at the shaft at the back which opened to the sky hundreds of feet up.

Making her way across the soft sand to the other end of the beach, past a small island about to be cut off by the tide, she found a track running up between very steep sand dunes. Arriving somewhat breathlessly at the top, Sarah found herself once more on common ground on which were grazing four cows, two donkeys and a small pony which trotted over in the hope of getting something to eat. However Sarah's essentials had not included carrots or sugar lumps so the pony quickly lost interest. Sarah wandered over to a collection of large stones sunk into the ground which puzzled her until she realised that looking down on them, they spelt EIRE. It was a legacy from WW2, an indication to pilots both allied and axis that they were now over neutral Irish territory.

Looking across the common land, she saw in the distance a lake with what appeared to be a tumbledown boat house at its Northern tip. In the other direction, about half a mile away was a gate, past which a road ran towards the entrance to a caravan park. She walked briskly to the road and followed it to the caravan park. With a light heart she practically skipped up to the door of a small house just inside and to the left of the entrance.

An elderly lady came to the door, obviously surprised, and not expecting callers.

"Come in dear" she said, "we don't get many visitors as early in the season as this. The kettle is just boiled, I'm sure you could take a cup of tea!".

Mrs Boyce had run the caravan park since her husband died. She had a large family but only two had remained in the area.

The two girls saw her regularly and their husbands could be relied upon to do any heavy work that was needed. During the season she employed some casual labour. She was a kind woman, a mother figure and Sarah felt very comfortable with her. Without, she hoped, being too antisocial, she fended Mrs Boyce's questions. Yes, she would like to rent a caravan for a couple of months. No, there was no husband to join her. Yes, she was here for a rest, to read and do some hill walking. No, she did not feel lonely or need company. Yes, she would feel free to use the house phone because there was no reception for mobiles. No, she would not use the shuttle bus which ran into Duncarry every other morning, she preferred the walk and no she did not need the services of the mobile shop which called twice per week.

She agreed a short lease on an elderly static caravan set on the edge of the site just above a sandy bay.

"Strange girl" said Mrs Boyce to Mrs Fegan the next morning as they sat in the rusting red minibus which made the journey into Duncarry. "Pleasant, but withdrawn. Good looking, I'm surprised there is no husband".

"Maybe she is one of those loosebins we hear about" said Mrs Fegan. "There were two in a tent in Murphy's Field last year, always holding hands and cuddling".

"I think they are called lesbians, but it's no odds, what people do is their own affair, but this woman is very much on her own".

"What's her name?"

"Rose Blaney".

"I wonder if she is related to the Milford Blaneys", mused Mrs Fegan

"Unlikely, she is from the North and has a bit of an English accent".

Sarah, for her part, felt safe in her anonymity. On her walks she saw very few people, a few farmers out on the hills collecting sheep and once, a party of walkers crossed the horizon about half a mile from her. During one of her walks she had noticed an isolated Mountain pub and decided, as a treat, to visit it at the end of the week. Not speaking or hearing talk was taking its toll.

CHAPTER 6

Sarah's Story

Sarah's early life had not been happy. Expelled from two of Ulster's Grammar Schools for smoking and general defiance, she found herself at sixteen with no qualifications and no job. She also had a liking for unsuitable boyfriends, bad boys from across the tracks. She really ran wild and nothing her sister Claire or her parents said or did made any difference.

She was very pretty, with a powerful sexual aura, and had little trouble bending men to her will. She was generally unpopular with other females, who feared for their husbands and boyfriends, as her wandering eye identified any weakness in a relationship which she could exploit.

By the time she was eighteen she reckoned that Belfast was too small a pool and went to London in the company of one of the unsuitable boyfriends. She didn't tell her parents or Claire that she was going. They were left to find out from friends and from her father's credit card company, pointing out that his credit card had reached its limit of five thousand pounds in just two days. It had gone to London as well!

It's not that Sarah was bad - just amoral. She simply took what she wanted but didn't intend hurting or annoying anyone. If someone was annoyed or hurt that was for them to deal with.

In London, her longhaired, slim looks made her an instant success. She appeared in the pages of both fashion and glamour magazines and made at least two short films for which few clothes were needed. She was on the guest list of all the parties given, and attended both huge extravaganzas and small, intimate evenings.

Of course she cut out all contact with her parents and sister. Part of the party circle, she rubbed shoulders with captains of industry, high earning professionals, politicians and minor foreign royalty. She didn't work as such but lived on her wits, occupying consecutively a number of expensive apartments supplied by male admirers.

However, by about 1995 things started to go wrong as her consumption of drugs increased. As her consumption rose, so also did her need for money, and with no job and no qualifications, she had only one thing of value to sell – herself. She had always enjoyed sex. Getting paid for it, she thought, would be a bonus. The only problem was that before she chose who she fucked, now that was a luxury she literally couldn't afford.

Many men were kind, thoughtful, grateful and generous but there was also the large minority, the mean, sadistic, spiteful men who really hated women and wanted to violate them in the most painful ways available. They were only interested in humiliation and Sarah did feel humiliated. After a particularly bad session with two middle Eastern businessmen, in real pain from their assault, she actually took an overdose in the hotel bedroom, having gone down to the hotel shop for a number of packets of paracetamol. However, the room had only been booked until 8.00pm and when the maids came in to change the bed linen, they found her and called an ambulance. She was released from hospital after twenty-four hours. It was shortly after this, in a fit of self loathing, that she began to cut herself. At first it gave her some relief, made her feel she was paying for being bad, but addiction took over and soon her arms and thighs were a mass of scars, which, along with the array of needle marks did not endear her to the better clients who wanted the pretence that they were really spending time with the woman next door who was thoroughly enjoying their skills.

Things went rapidly downhill and, with her income from prostitution now severely reduced, she began to deal in drugs which soon brought her to the attention of the police. Convictions followed, and things got so bad she was even convicted of soliciting in the street. Do anything for twenty five pounds, she offered. The luxury apartments had long gone and by the millennium she was living in a homeless persons' hostel. A number of suicide attempts followed.

When she regained consciousness after the last attempt, she opened her eyes to see a tall, well built, softly spoken, coloured man looking down at her.

"You are so handsome, am I in heaven?" she said. At least that's what Tom later told her she had said. She couldn't actually remember!

Tom was a part-time volunteer drug counsellor involved in a new, one–to-one rehabilitation programme being pioneered by the hospital. He was assigned to Sarah and felt an immediate affinity with her, recognising her vulnerability. A couple of days after their first meeting, Tom was explaining the outline of the programme.

"Sarah, I could go on talking about this until the cows come home but in reality, the most important question is. Do you really want to kick the habit?"

Sarah took a week to decide. The answer was 'Yes' and Tom said he would guide and support her through the nightmare of the long, difficult, soul destroying and physically exhausting process.

He was kind, loving, generous, supportive, understanding and forgiving, but he was also strict and realistic. It wasn't easy; there were rows, backsliding, and abuse. Sarah said horrible things to him and sometimes attacked him, but he bore it all with patience and good humour. By the end of the year Sarah was dry and in love with Tom.

That was when she re-established contact with her sister Claire, both her parents having died in the intervening years. She and Tom made a number of visits to Belfast and Sarah seemed blissfully happy, although there was no talk of either marriage or children. Nor was Claire aware at this time that Tom was working for the Security Services and that Sarah would soon be as well.

When Tom died in the bomb explosion in the underground, Sarah could not face continuing with her undercover work in spite of being the guinea pig for a new surveillance system. Much of it had already been fitted, but there were plans to record images through a micro camera built into a contact lens. Sarah didn't feel up to it in the circumstances and her superiors sympathetically agreed. She returned to Belfast for a long recovery. It wasn't that she was particularly close to her sister but she needed, not so much her support, but rather to know it was there, and she was scared if she continued to live in London, she might be tempted back to her old ways.

She felt she had settled down well, her job was satisfying if not demanding, which suited her well on her return from London and fortunately, she had no contact with friends from her early wild period in Belfast. In fact, she saw very few people and felt none the worse for that. At work she was reserved but joined in with the conversations, although she had little to contribute on topics of church, family and local gossip. Really she felt as if she had come from another world (which she had). Compared to her, they had led such sheltered lives. However, she was not about to enlighten them, she felt they would not stand the shock.

Her job would not keep her interested much longer. Already

the traces of boredom had set in and now, well recovered, she felt she was ready to undertake something more demanding. If it wasn't for the fees she would even consider university as a mature student. Still, there was always the Open University.

CHAPTER 7

"What we need is a lucky break" said Commander Harris of Counter Terrorist Command. "This woman can't just disappear off the face of the earth. How exactly did you approach her?" he demanded of Frank Burns, the senior liaison officer acting between the police and M15. Burns squirmed uncomfortably in his chair.

Harris didn't like getting nowhere. His temper, never good at the best of times, was even shorter.

"Get this fucking room cleaned. All of you lazy bastards get off your fat arses and at least pretend to be doing something. Linton, take Smyth and go through her house with a fine tooth comb. Speak to her sister first, we'll keep you informed from this end".

"Excuse me Sir, what exactly are we looking for?" asked Smyth.

"What the fuck do you think we're looking for? Evidence as to where she's gone, Jesus, does everything have to be spelled out for you"?

Sergeant Smyth had also intended to ask about the equipment which was supposed to be missing, but on reflection, thought better of it and the pair left avoiding Harris' eye.

Burns came rushing through the door. "We have her" he cried.

"Good work" said Harris, "who picked her up and where?"

"Er...not quite, I mean we have her on video".

"I should have known" said Harris, "... tell us what you have".

"Spotted in Central Station boarding the Londonderry train at 11.10 am".

"Try the Derry tapes".

"In hand Sir".

"Get on to Linton and Smyth and get them to ask the sister if Sarah knows anyone in Derry".

The two detectives in question got the news just as they approached Claire's house.

"Are we still pretending to be from Missing Persons?" asked Smyth.

"I think so, leave it to me".

Five minutes after their visit, Claire was on the phone to Mike and Alan. "Derry was her destination according to the police". "Unless she's got off in Ballymena" said Alan.

"Don't be stupid, no one is that desperate" said Mike.

"No they also have video evidence of her leaving the Derry station" said Claire.

"What's the point of us just following the police line?" enquired Alan. "We should either back off or take a different approach".

"Sherlock Holmes never backed off".

"Watson didn't have Parkinson's".

"Stop feeling sorry for yourself. You are as fit as a fiddle, just get on with it. Remember we are helping a damsel in distress".

"Hoping to get one into distress, more likely in your case".

"Seriously though, we have to go on now. She is obviously going to cross the border into Donegal and the PSNI have no jurisdiction there, they will not be able to follow".

In King's Barracks, Holywood, Commander Harris was expressing the same sentiment. "If she goes over the border it's a matter for the Garda Siochana and they aren't likely to take a missing person matter too seriously".

"Can we take the train to Derry?" asked Mike.

"Why?" said Alan.

"I like trains, I like the freedom, the buffet car, the drinks, the meals".

"When were you last on a train?"

"Why?"

"Because trains aren't like that any longer. However, they do have wonderful toilets. They open up wide and look like a palace. The only problem is, if you don't press the right button to lock them, they'll open up when you are in the middle of a crap. Still, it's all about breaking down inhibitions".

"One of my first jobs was to walk along the roofs of the carriages in the station, filling the toilet cisterns, used to put frogs in sometimes or even the odd goldfish. Ah... those were the days" said Mike. "By the way do you think the old Merc is up to a trip to Donegal?"

"Hasn't let us down yet".

Mike recalled these words as they sat on the scenic Glenshane Pass watching the clouds, birds, cattle and sheep moving which the Merc most certainly was not!

The car had behaved badly. First of all it had been slow to start, not unusual in a 20 year old car, but perhaps it should have been taken as a warning. En route the car lost power at times, embarrassing to be sitting at 25 mph on the single carriageway to Derry with an ever lengthening queue forming behind.

"All those people will think we're a couple of old fools" said Mike

"They wouldn't be far wrong" said Alan, struggling to keep the car moving.

Suddenly it sprang into life and Alan accelerated up to 80 mph.

"Maybe we can drive the bugs out. It hasn't been on a long journey for quite a time, the engine is probably just choked up".

Twenty minutes later the queue had formed again.

"We can't go on like this" said Mike. "We are almost at walking pace".

However, the problem was solved for them when the engine died completely. Luckily they were within pushing distance of a lay-by and, assisted by two young men from a white van, they got the car off the road.

Five minutes later, with the bonnet up and the two men peering at the engine, not having a clue what they were looking for, they heard a car draw up. Mike looked out from under the bonnet.

"Bloody police" he whispered, "what the fuck do they want?"

"Afternoon gentlemen, we are just investigating reports of severe congestion on the road".

"Bloody tractors" said Mike, "should be banned from public roads".

"Looks as if you are in trouble here" said the other Constable.

"We're not quite sure what the problem is" said Alan.

"Do you belong to any of the motoring organisations?" asked the first Constable, walking round the car, checking the tax disc and the wear on the tyres.

"Oh yes, I'm in the AA" said Alan. "I had forgotten all about it".

"OK" said the Constable "we'll send them out to you. Take care as you go" he said on leaving.

"Told you we should've used the train".

"Sure you're too proud to use your Pensioners Pass anyway".

"The AA will sort it".

"Never sorted me out" said Mike.

"The Automobile Association has a much higher success rate in fixing cars than Alcoholics Anonymous has in fixing Alcoholics!"

"Could do with a drink at the minute" said Mike.

"Saw a pub about five miles back".

"Maybe the AA chap could nip over and collect a few beers".

"Well, you can ask, here they are".

The yellow AA van pulled up alongside and a dapper young

mechanic, dressed in spotless overalls, stepped out.

"Fucking great" said Mike, "we get the tailor's dummy".

"Bit old, gentlemen" was the AA mechanics greeting.

"Us or the car" enquired Mike. "Are you people not supposed to salute?"

"When did you last contact the AA Granda?"

"Never mind the lip, just fix the fucking car."

"I don't appreciate bad language. I can just drive on you know".

"Just ignore him" said Alan as Mike began a stream of invective in Swedish.

"He's not swearing at me in a foreign language is he?"

"Of course not, he's really rather shy and is just complimenting you on your turn out."

"We do try to dress well" said the mechanic, " I see the problem and I'll send someone out from the Derry garage when I get back".

"Wait a minute, what happened to roadside repairs?" asked Alan.

"Cars are too complicated now mate. Nothing we can do when they breakdown, it's a main dealer's job, they have all the computer equipment".

Mike came round the side of the van with the wheel brace from the boot in his hand.

"I have a better idea" he said with a dangerous look in his eyes. "You stay here with the car and we'll take the van into Derry".

"You are not serious" said the mechanic.

"Indeed we are" said Alan "what a wonderful idea".

The young mechanic's perma-tan lost three shades.

"Hold on" he said. "I can give them a ring, tell them it's an A1 emergency and they'll be here in twenty minutes".

"Good lad. I knew you had initiative". said Mike. "Now just stay in your van until the cavalry arrive, then I'll give you back your keys", he said with a smile.

Twenty minutes later a real mechanic turned up, replaced a black box control unit, and the Mercedes purred into life.

"Those little black boxes are magic" said Alan.

"They're also expensive" said the mechanic. "That'll be two hundred and seventy pounds please".

"Put it down to expenses" said Mike as the car pulled back onto the road.

"Have you forgotten Holmes, due to your big heart and even bigger libido, we're working for nothing".

"You'll get your reward in Heaven".

"If I continue to keep company with you I'll never get there".

Tired with their exertions, the two elderly gentlemen decided to spend the night in Derry before following the trail to God knows where.

"We are a bit pushed for space" said the assistant Manageress at the Foyleview Hotel. "There's a business convention on in the city and nearly every room is taken. However, have a drink and your meal and we'll sort something out". She seemed to be under some pressure.

"Are you on your own?" asked Mike.

"The Manager is off ill and the receptionist has not turned up, but we'll get through it" she replied. "I'll sort out your accommodation".

She was about fifty years old, dyed blonde hair, a bit overweight, heavily made up but with a real charm and a friendly manner. She could have been a role model for the position she held.

The hotel itself was old, a bit worn, but clean. The reception and lounge areas were covered in photographs of the U.S. Forces in Derry in the 1940s. There were also photographs of the surrender of the German Atlantic Submarine fleet in 1945 which took place in Derry. An elderly man noticed their interest.

"I can remember as a boy all the troops in Derry, before the D

Day Invasion. Lough Foyle was an important staging post for the troops".

"Funny coincidence" said Alan "Bangor, where we live, was also a major staging post for the D Day Landings".

The elderly man's face lit up at the possibility of an audience.

"There sure was a lot of excitement in those days. I can remember the hunt for the Bismarck and the survivors coming ashore. The ship's cat came with them and it lived with us for many years".

"Did it mew German?" asked Mike.

The man looked puzzled.

"Ignore him" said Alan "he goes like that at times. Can we buy you a drink?" he asked moving towards the bar.

"Why thank you" said the old gentleman, "I'll have a pint of Guinness and a double whiskey as a chaser. I don't often get a drink bought to me these days".

"No bloody wonder if that's your normal order" thought Mike.

"So, you're a Derry man born and bred?" asked Alan, his wallet considerably lighter.

"Indeed I am, man and boy. I remember the war days like they were yesterday. All the ships in Lough Foyle, and the soldiers - the Yanks here before being shipped off to Europe. They had so much money to spend on the girls, us locals didn't stand a chance".

The bar walls continued the war theme with more photographs. Generals in dress uniform; officers and men in both formal and informal poses; American divisions marching through Derry, aircraft and aircrews at local bases and always, ships of all descriptions.

"The hotel owners must be very interested in the war?" ventured Mike.

"Not really" said the old man, "It's to attract the tourists. Some of the photos have nothing to do with Derry. For example, look at that photo of a Sunderland Flying Boat, it was based down on

Lough Erne in Fermanagh. I can remember the excitement when one of them found the Bismarck. I told you, didn't I, that some of her crew were brought ashore here?"

"Indeed you did" said Mike, his eyes glazing over.

"Very nice to have met you" said Alan, "But we have to go and eat now".

"Oh, I'm sorry about that, I could've had another drink and told you some more about the war", said the old man wistfully eyeing his empty glasses.

"Maybe another time" said Mike.

A couple of hours later, fortified by stiff brandies after a solid meal, they made their way to the room they had been allocated.

"Only one bed, we can't both sleep in that, people will think we're gay" announced Mike.

"They probably think it anyway. I'm so tired I could sleep anywhere".

"Well I'm not sleeping here" said Mike as he stormed out.

Alan went to sleep immediately, waking at five am wondering if he should go and look for Mike in case he was crushed up in one of the lounge chairs. He considered carefully, then turned over and went back to sleep.

Waking again at seven, he got washed, shaved and dressed. He made his way along the corridor to find Mike emerging from another room, saying thank you to someone still inside.

"Who was that?" asked Alan.

"Just the Assistant Manageress. They had no more rooms left so she kindly shared hers. Purely a business transaction".

"Judging from the smile on your face a very satisfactory transaction" said Alan enviously.

"Had to prove we're not a gay couple", beamed Mike, "now let's have breakfast".

Two hours later the Merc was on the new Derry bridge and

Holmes and Watson were deciding which route to follow.

"This is where we need inspiration" said Alan, "remember she has no car".

"Bit like us then".

"Give over, the car is fine and wont let us down again".

"Letterkenny".

"What?"

"Letterkenny is where she went to".

"What makes you so certain?"

"Look at it like this. She arrives late in Derry, she wants over the border quickly, Letterkenny has by far and away the best bus service so she takes the bus to Letterkenny".

"O.K. " said Alan, "Letterkenny it is".

CHAPTER 8

Meanwhile back in Belfast, Detectives Linton and Smyth had spent over three hours going through Sarah's house but found nothing out of the ordinary, apart from a file of medical records which they were sitting looking at. The records were very comprehensive, dealing mostly with drug rehabilitation and neurological matters, but also contained surgical records which seemed to refer to cosmetic procedures.

"Why are the records here?" asked the Sergeant.

"I have a feeling this is drifting into MI5 territory, far too much secrecy for my liking" said Linton. "Let's talk to the nosey neighbour again".

Fifteen minutes later they were ensconced in Lily's front room with the obligatory cup of tea.

"But you said you were Estate Agents, I have told everyone that".

"We may have inadvertently given that impression but we are conducting enquiries into the disappearance of your neighbour Sarah Scott".

"Do you think something has happened to her?" asked Lily, unable to contain her excitement.

"We have no reason to believe anything is wrong".

"Then why all the fuss?" said Lily "and if you are not Estate Agents who were the other two men viewing the house?"

Both detectives straightened up.

"And who were they?" asked Linton.

"They said they were here to look over the house for a friend.

They had a key with them".

"Description" asked Smyth.

"Well one of them you couldn't miss, he was big with a very fancy jacket, white trousers and trainers. The other was small, well dressed but seemed to shake and stagger a bit. They both had white hair. Oh, the small one had a sort of country accent, whereas the big one was definitely from Belfast".

After a few minutes more questioning, it was obvious that Lily had no additional information to provide so Inspector Linton got to his feet.

"Many thanks for all your help and for the tea. Perhaps if you see anyone about the house you would give me a ring" he said passing her his card.

Back in the car the two detectives looked at each other.

"Who do you think the other two men were?" asked Smyth.

"I don't know but I have a fair idea who will know. Let's go and pay another visit to Claire".

"But I was at my wits' end and I felt no notice was being taken of anything I said" protested Claire. "You weren't doing much and I couldn't afford a proper private detective".

"That's all we need, a couple of geriatric idiots running amok and getting in everyone's way. " grunted Linton. "Have you any idea where they might be now?"

"I am afraid I told them about the video of the Derry train sighting, they were going to follow her tracks".

"Train tracks, very good" said Smyth immediately wilting under a baleful look from his superior.

"Well what's done is done" sighed Linton, "I suppose we should get back to base and face the music. The Boss won't be happy".

Caught in the rush hour traffic, the journey back to Holywood was slow. Inspector Linton turned over the evidence in his mind.

If she crossed the border into Donegal it became a matter for the Garda Siochana and the Commander would not be pleased. Although there was a high level of co-operation between the PSNI and the Garda Siochana, each liked to keep its own secrets and each had secrets to keep. Since the commander had not given his own team very much information, it was unlikely he would give more to his Garda counterpart. Then there was the shadowy world of MI5, where did they fit in? Where was Burns' interest in all of this? He would bet that Burns would be interested in, and understand, the medical records.

Commander Harris wasn't in a good mood but it had nothing to do with their inadequate detective work. Rather, it was because he had just been informed that the case had now become a joint police/MI5 enquiry. He thought very little of Burns and decided that with the last wave of police redundancies coming up in the near future, it just might be time to call it a day.

Burns for his part, was dismissive of Linton and Smyth but not of the medical files – he tucked them carefully inside his briefcase.

"Should we have those two old duffers picked up before they leave Derry?" asked Linton.

The thought seemed to amuse Burns, "Those two old men will be lucky to find their way out of Derry never mind find the missing woman".

He was closer to the truth than he knew. Leaving Derry, Mike and Alan decided to follow the side roads, the better to enjoy the scenery. Coming to a cross roads they faced a 'Road Closed' sign directly in front of them, barring their progress. Pointing to the left and to the right were two identical signs, each saying 'Diversion'. That had been half an hour ago and, in the absence of any other signs, they were now hopelessly lost.

"That's the third time we have passed that barn, not a criticism, only an observation" remarked Mike.

Attempts to ask for directions had led to such contradictory advice that their confusion was now even greater. It was with some embarrassment that they passed, for the second time, the last man they had asked for directions. They waved manically at him as though their erratic passage was part of a well planned excursion. He viewed their progress with baffled amazement.

"We can always ring the AA" suggested Mike.

"Perhaps not" said Alan, "Ah, I think I now know where we are", he said confidently taking a sharp left turn into a farmyard.

"Did they not teach you any navigational skills in the Forces?" enquired Alan.

"Of course they did" answered Mike "but I have to wait until night time when I can use the North Star to get my bearings".

From the farmhouse and outbuildings a motley array of figures emerged, an old lady dressed in black carrying a blackthorn walking stick, a middle-aged man dressed for the milking parlour, a woman, presumably his wife, who had obviously been feeding calves from the milk buckets she still carried, a teenager who looked, and smelt, as if he had been spreading slurry all morning, which actually he had, and the younger children looking shyly about before playing noughts and crosses on the dirty back panel of the car.

"I wonder if you can help us" asked Alan. "We are trying to get to Letterkenny but have taken a wrong turning".

"More than one, I would say" remarked the farmer.

"If I was going to Letterkenny I wouldn't start from here" contributed the teenager, helpfully.

"Best go by Nearycross" said Granny.

"Ah now that would not be best for the roads are so bad down there" said the calf feeding woman, "you would be better taking the road through Larkleigh".

"I tell you what is best, we will direct you to the high crossroads where the road is closed and there are diversion signs" said the farmer. "You can't go wrong from there".

"Dear God let me die" whispered Alan.

"The sound of an over revving engine could be heard in the distance. I have a far better idea" said the woman suddenly, "that's the post van coming. This is his last stop before he goes back to Letterkenny, sure all you have to do is follow him. He's a bit nervous, so I'll talk to him in case he thinks you are trying to hijack him".

"Brilliant" said Mike, turning to Alan "why didn't you think of that?"

The post van entered the yard at speed, the gravel kicked up by its tyres. Driving straight past them, it skidded to a stop by the back door. The farmer's wife went over to the van, took the mail from the driver's window and had a brief conversation with the postman. She walked back to the Mercedes. "It's alright" she said, "you can follow him".

The post van left the yard the way it had entered, with tyres spinning and a fine hail of gravel and dust being thrown up against the Merc's bonnet and windscreen.

"Bloody fantastic, now we have to follow someone practising for the Donegal International Rally" said Mike.

The road was narrow but the post van driver seemed to believe he had right of way. Alan kept behind him, but not too close, so that if the van hit anything he would have time to pull up.

The postman was obviously well known in the area, motorists they met took to the ditches for safety, and even the farm dogs held back from running out at the van. Alan cast a glance at Mike who was demonstrating the forty shades of green.

"Don't you be sick in the car"

"Slow down can't you".

"I can't, we might lose him".

"If we don't, I will lose everything I have eaten in the last twelve hours".

"Stick your head out of the window".

A side-ways drift nearly did it for Mike, but thankfully the outskirts of Letterkenny were now in sight. Approaching the main road, the post van stopped. Alan stopped behind it and walked forward to thank the postman. Imagine his surprise when instead of looking at a young tearaway, as he had expected, he was actually looking at a little old man in a fluorescent jacket and long-peaked baseball cap, wearing bottle-end glasses and a hearing aid.

"That was a quick journey" said Alan.

"Sure I was going slow to let you keep up".

"What about the cars that nearly drove off the road to avoid us?"

"I never saw that, of course I've tunnel vision syndrome".

"Well, thanks anyway" said Alan.

"You're welcome" said the postman, taking off again in his customary style, nearly causing an articulated lorry to jack-knife in its attempt to avoid him.

CHAPTER 9

The pillars of light over Sheephaven Bay were amazing. It seemed to her that God had opened a trap door in heaven for a quick look at what was happening below.

Rose Blaney, she had to pause before remembering the name she was currently using, felt really well. The isolation and exercise seemed to agree well with her. She found it hard to believe that twelve years ago she was a cocaine, heroin, amphetamine popping junkie.

Those were the bad, dark days. She shuddered at the memory. If it hadn't been for Tom, beautiful, loving, understanding Tom she would be long dead. The years spent with him had been the happiest in her life and the fact that they were working together was an added bonus. He had been her saviour, she would never have believed that any man could have had such an influence over her. She missed him really badly at times, now being one of them. How he would have loved the wildness of Donegal. She so wished he was with her now, but she was comforted by his memory and the feeling that his spirit was all around her, enveloping her as she stood there on top of the small mountain looking at the breathtaking panorama spread before her. From the distinctive Salt Mountain with Glen Lough lying below it, over to Muckish with Errigle lurking behind it, across the flat top of Bloody Foreland to Tory, that magical, mystical island lost in the western mists of the Atlantic. Below her, two long beaches of golden sand, totally deserted and a small harbour with only a couple of small boats moored to the quay. 'What a wonderful picture' she thought.

Of course she was realistic enough to recognise that at least one reason for her good form was that today was gift day, the present she'd promised herself, the visit to the Mountain Pub. Not that she was expecting much life in it at this time of year.

She made her way back to the caravan. Although the van was old, it really was in a beautiful location. Parked between sand dunes for shelter, it overlooked the sandy bay beneath but was not overlooked itself. What a romantic spot she thought. In the summer time you could lie out naked and soak up the sun's rays.

"Rose, Rose" she heard with surprise her name being called, then she realised it was Mrs Boyce. She walked back between the sand dunes to meet her.

"Just wanted to let you know that the postman will take any letters you might want to post".

"Thanks, I'll remember that".

"And if you need to phone use the one in the house. Such a pity you can't get reception for mobiles here".

"It doesn't matter, I don't have a mobile anyway".

"Do you not need one for work?"

"No, I'm a freelance writer, I don't have to be at anyone's beck and call".

Mrs Boyce retreated, defeated once again.

"You can get nothing out of her" she said to Mrs Fegan on the bus the next morning.

"Maybe there's nothing to get".

"Something is not right, mark my words. A young woman like that on her own. She is running away from something or someone". She made a mental note to ask Tony who drove the mobile shop if he had heard anything. Tony was usually good for a bit of gossip.

Dressed comfortably in black jeans and a black polo neck sweater, Sarah pulled on her long mountain anorak and headed for the pub in the hills. It was a fair step, but she realised there would be little point in arriving before 9pm. The last thing she wanted was an empty pub and a talkative barman.

When she entered the pub it was quiet, but not deserted. A couple of young fellows were playing darts and a mixed group of young people was milling around a pool table. Three elderly men conversed in Irish in a corner at the end of the bar.

"What will you be having?" asked the barman.

"A pint of Guinness please, and do you do food?" she asked hopefully.

"Sure" he said producing a basic menu, all items on which she noted were microwaveable. Still, what could you expect?

"You're from the North then?" he said, but there is a trace of another accent there. I'm good on accents, I would guess London".

"Yes I have spent some time there," said Sarah before turning away from the bar and taking a seat in a dark corner beside a door which, she assumed, led into a store room.

"Have you decided on what to eat?" asked the barman.

"Could I have a burger and chips in about an hour's time?" she asked. "I just want to enjoy my pint and read for a bit first".

"Not much light for reading where you're sitting, would you not like to move over there where there is more light?"

"Not necessary, I use this" said Sarah producing something like a large mobile phone or small notebook. "It's called a Kindle and it's a kind of electronic book, like a little computer actually, you can carry about hundreds of books on it, each page comes up on screen and it has its own light".

"I've heard of them but never seen one" said the barman, "what will they come up with next?"

In actual fact the seat she had chosen was really very comfortable. She could lean back against the wooden partition and, from a secluded position, observe everything going on in the bar.

Above the fireplace was an old ship's wheel. Candles had been roughly inserted and it was bedecked with the County football ribbons. Below it was a model ship in a glass display case. To the right were some old pieces of farming equipment tightly fastened to the wall. Charts showing Atlantic fish and pictures of ships adorned the other walls.

She noticed a large plate of sandwiches being prepared behind the bar, obviously more customers were expected.

Her attention then drifted to the three old men who were speaking in Irish at the end of the bar. She guessed they would all be in their 70s, thin, wiry, mountain men. They wore mismatched jackets and trousers from old suits, and shirts which had seen too few washes over too many years. They all wore working boots. Their facial features lined and leathery, shaped by years of herding sheep on the mountainside, were a series of valleys and ridges, producing some of the most distinctive countenances she had ever seen. Compared with the young pool players, they looked like tribal patriarchs, all seeing, all knowing and the mellifluous tones of their native language caressed by their soft Donegal accents, touched her soul. She guessed they were all bachelors, there was something about them which proclaimed independence and self sufficiency, yet called out for care.

She had her beef burger and chips with her second pint of Guinness, every bit as well drawn and smooth as the first. She did miss a cigarette, however, and was actually considering buying a packet when the bar door opened. A young man, probably about thirty, wearing a black overcoat over a black tee-shirt and jeans strode over to the bar.

"Everything O. K. Mick? Nothing out of the ordinary?"

"All quiet Sean, never anything happening at this time of year".

Sean quickly scanned the bar.

"Do many of the old ones still speak Irish?" he asked

"Only a few, sure everything the young are interested in is in English".

"If I had my way they would bloody well have to speak it" said Sean.

"Maybe someday you will".

Sarah listened from the shadows thinking what a lovely man the new visitor was. She had shown no interest in a man since Tom's death but now with two pints of Guinness she felt distinct stirrings of interest.

However the young man passed her without even noticing her and went through the door into what Rose could now see was not a store room, but a compact room set up for a meeting with a table, about eight chairs, paper, an overhead projector and a flip chart. Obviously this was where the sandwiches would end up. Sarah checked her watch, nearly 10.00pm, late for a meeting, but the Irish do keep late nights. She'd just taken the first bite from the burger when she heard the sound of cars arriving. The door opened and eight men ranging from mid 20s to late 60s walked in. If their ages were varied, so too was their dress. One man, grey haired, mid 40s dressed in a dark suit, caught her eye. Well set up she thought, intelligent, confident with that interesting whiff of evil, just the type she had traditionally gone for. However, he and the others passed without taking her under their notice.

Well, thought Sarah, this corner is either darker than I thought, or the old pulling power has gone. She leaned back against the partition and to her surprise found that if she turned her ear to the panel behind her, the tunnel of wood created by the construction of the alcove actually acted as a speaker effect, conveying the discussion from the room with remarkable clarity. It acted like one of those ear trumpets she had seen in old films. At first she paid little attention to what was going on but slowly in her mind unconscious patterns began to emerge.

The penny dropped when the discussion focussed on the Omagh bomb. She was listening to the leaders of a dissident republican terrorist group talking and, worse, laughing about past successes and laying plans for future attacks. She sat mesmerised and horrified as they discussed the detail of the Omagh bombing. Suddenly she remembered her work with security and the technological additions she had been fitted with. Tentatively she found the hidden switch at the base of her thumb and pressed. A slight tremor passed through her breast and she knew the device was active. She curled up in the alcove, her ear and breast against the panel, listening attentively as she pretended to be reading from the Kindle.

For the next hour and a half she heard them planning their activities for the next twelve months. Ignoring obvious exaggerations and flights of fancy, it was a horrendous picture of potential mayhem and death, all in the cause of a united Ireland which no one who was sane would want achieved by these methods.

She listened to the plans to attack police stations, government buildings and banks, the use of snipers in London, car bombs in Birmingham, the possibility of assisting the Islamic extremists. As the discussion turned to the planning of immediate attacks on identified targets, including probable dates for specific targets, she began to feel physically ill. The potential for human horror devastated and disgusted her. One thing was certain, this information had to find its way to the security forces both North and South of the border.

The barman was starting to tidy up. At the pool table, body language indicated who was walking home with whom and the young people tripped out, talking and laughing into the night.

The three elderly Irish speakers moved to the centre of the bar for a last drink.

The planning in the room had ceased and with the arrival of the sandwiches conversation turned from murder, mayhem and destruction, to gaelic football, hurling and women. The barman turned on the main lights and Rose got unsteadily to her feet. At that moment the door of the small room opened and the grey haired, grey suited man she had noticed on his arrival, walked over to the bar.

"That's fine Mick, a good night's work. We will be leaving shortly but let's have a whiskey for everyone before we go".

He turned to re-enter the room, this time noticing Sarah. He gave her a glance, then a longer stare.

Perhaps I haven't lost it after all, thought Rose before remembering with disgust what he had been discussing minutes earlier.

She stepped out into a beautiful moonlight night, but was too shocked and horrified by what she had heard to notice the beauty of the evening. She stumbled back to the caravan. She was certain about one thing. The information must be passed on. However, first she needed sleep.

Meanwhile in the planning room, the plate of sandwiches demolished, everyone seemed in good humour save one.

"What in Christ's name is the matter Francis?" asked Joe across the table, but he got no reply. One night cap had become two, then three, but Francis had become silent and withdrawn. He was moody, they knew that, but things had gone really well and many of his ideas and plans had been accepted.

"Jesus Christ" he said loudly.

CHAPTER 10

Commander Harris knew it wouldn't be an easy meeting. Around the table were Burns from MI5, the Garda Deputy Commissioner, Michael Burke and Halford from the Southern anti-terrorist intelligence unit.

"Gentlemen" said Burke, speaking first to emphasise that he was the senior officer present, "let us lay our cards on the table. We know you've lost a valuable piece of espionage equipment believed to be in the possession of a Sarah Scott who may have run off with it to Donegal with the possible intention of selling it to the highest bidder. Agreed Halford?"

"Yes Sir that is how we read it. We believe that the airport near Bunbeg will be used by a private plane to bring in foreign buyers. The whole thing has been planned by a dissident organisation with whom Ms Scott has allied for personal gain. We also know she had a very expensive lifestyle in London a few years ago and it is our belief that she was recruited by the dissidents at that time and told to continue working for MI5. She was given this piece of expensive and technically very advanced equipment just about four weeks ago whereupon she fled with it to Donegal".

"What a load of bollocks" said Burns. "You call that intelligence. Do you even know what has gone missing?"

Burke and Halford looked at each other uncomfortably.

"We haven't actually determined..." started Burke.

"It's a fucking woman" said Harris.

"You're not serious" said Burke "that missing person stuff

was genuine, we assumed she was carrying a newly developed speciality weapon".

"What weapon?" demanded Burns. "Who ever mentioned a weapon?"

"We assumed that it was one of those tiny personal lasers which can pass undetected through security checks and which spies therefore could use for personal security". said Halford.

"Well it's not and I don't even know if such a thing exists" said Burns.

"Let us fill you in on a few details" said Harris.

Two hours later Harris and Burns left the building.

"Did you ever hear such a load of shite?" said Harris. "I don't know how you cope with all this nonsense, all the lies and intrigues on a daily basis".

"You get used to it. At least they will now help us look for the woman".

"Yes but you know how sensitive they are. Don't stand on any toes if you can help it".

Meanwhile, back on the road with Holmes and Watson.

"Fastest growing town in Europe" said Mike, "or at least it was before the recession. Used to do a bit of business here, not totally above board".

"Were you ever involved in any business which was totally legitimate?"

"Well, there was the Sports Academy and Golf Driving Range".

"Ah yes, all those ladies you helped with their swing" said Alan caustically.

"Don't know why you're so humped" said Mike. "Haven't I brought you safely to Letterkenny?"

"I'll never forget those finely honed navigation skills, now perhaps you could give us a clue as to where we should go from here?"

"Elementary my dear Watson, elementary, but while we're thinking, let's have some lunch".

"Put yourself in her shoes," Alan said as they sipped coffee after a very mediocre lunch. "She wants away from people, somewhere secluded".

Alan's mobile phone bleeped. He answered and listened intently, punctuating the silence with a few encouraging noises. "Thanks Claire" he said and rang off.

"Well, this is interesting" he said. "Claire was visited again by those two policemen who seem to be taking the matter much more seriously. In fact, Claire said they were really quite hyped up. She's scared that they may now believe that something has happened to Sarah. She certainly thought they'd moved up a gear. Oh... and they know we're on the case!"

"They must be relieved by that" said Mike, "Now how the hell do we trace her from here? I think we should take the afternoon off, buy a nice bottle of wine, get some snacks and motor over to Portsalon for a picnic and indulge in some creative thinking".

"I think we have gone as far as we can" said Alan. "I'm not against the idea of a picnic, we might as well get some pleasure from the trip, we might be able to hire clubs and have a round of golf".

They were just outside a small supermarket and it seemed sensible that they should stock up for the afternoon. Mike made his way to the wine shelves at the back of the store. An open door led to a small yard in which was parked a mobile shop. The driver was talking to someone Mike guessed was the deputy manager.

"Terrible sad about old Joe Doherty" said the deputy manager. "Apparently he was dead for three days before anyone went to the house".

Mike was scanning the wine selection somewhat taken aback by the prices.

"He never seemed to need or want people near him" continued the assistant manager.

"Sure it takes all sorts" said the driver. "Only last week one of my customers was telling me about this good looking city girl who rented a caravan four weeks ago and has hardly been seen since. No contact with anyone at any time. It's my belief that she is trying to heal a broken heart".

"I'm surprised you're not down to help with the healing process" said the deputy manager.

"Away with you, sure I'm a happily married man".

"Aye, happy because of the girlfriend. Just like a mobile shop keeper to have his cake and eat it".

Although years of heavy drinking had killed off a fair number of brain cells, Mike could still put two and two together, and he quickly realised this could be their incredibly lucky break.

He spoke to the driver who had just loaded three boxes of wine into the mobile shop.

"I didn't know you could sell wine from a mobile shop" he said. As an icebreaker, a way to join in the conversation, it was a complete non-starter.

"I don't sell it, I swap it for euro".

Mike knew when he was being made a fool of and in his best Canadian accent said,

"Gee I was sure interested in what you were saying about the young woman staying on her own. I'm over from Canada doing a tour of the old family spots in Ireland and my niece e-mailed me to say she would be staying in Donegal for a few weeks, giving me the address where she would be staying. Of course, I forgot to print it out and bring it with me. It could just be that the woman you were speaking about could be my niece. Did you see what she looked like?"

"No I didn't see her".

"Ah she is beautiful, tall, dark haired; my sister, God rest her soul, thought the world of her. You have often heard me speak of them" he said to Alan who had drifted down to the back of the store to see what was happening.

"What are we talking about?" he enquired, quite thrown by Mike's Canadian accent.

"My sister Anne and her daughter Christine". "I was telling this gentleman I had foolishly left behind Christine's temporary address in Donegal".

"I don't know her address" said the mobile shop driver, "I just know that the woman who told me about her lives out at Sand Head at the top of the Ross Peninsula. But listen" he added, "you say she e-mailed you her address, you can go up the street to the internet café and call up your e-mails".

"I'm not very good on technology" said Mike, beginning to panic.

"No problem, I'll come and do it for you" said the van driver. "it'll be my good deed for the day".

"Don't worry" said Alan, stepping in quickly to rescue the floundering Mike. "I can manage it for him, old men never take easily to the new technology".

"Not like you" said the driver who was rapidly coming to like Mike and was feeling defensive for him.

Ignoring him, Alan said, "The internet café is a great idea, we never thought of it and it would be a shame if he missed his niece on this trip. He may not have many more" he said to the driver under his breath.

"Well, good luck. I hope you find her wherever she is" said the driver.

That was a bit of luck for them, he thought as he watched them disappear into the internet café and a bit of luck for me too, now I've a bit of gossip for Mrs Boyce. Strange though, he thought, he didn't think that Mrs Boyce's tenant had been called Christine. Still he'd never been very good with names.

"Do we have to go in here?" protested Mike, "it's full of young people".

"They'll not bite you" retorted Alan, "and it looks better that we do. We don't want to give him a clue that you were telling a pack of lies".

"I was dead worried when he suggested coming up with me".

"You've done well Holmes".

"Yes I did rather, the accent was good. We might be within a few hours of solving our first case. Should we ring Claire and let her know"?

"Better wait until we are sure. At the minute we are getting carried away with our own cleverness. Might not be our woman at all".

The pair were unusually quiet on the drive over to the Ross Peninsula, each lost in his own thoughts, wondering what to do if the identification proved positive. Would they confront her, tell her sister, or should they simply inform Claire that Sarah was safe and allow her her privacy?

Coming over the top of the mountain road, the Ross Peninsula spread out beneath them, its beaches sparkling in the sun. Alan pulled the car into a viewing area and they looked out, overwhelmed by the beauty of the scenery.

"Almost enough to make you religious" said Mike.

"I wouldn't go that far. Tell me Mike, if you had it all to do again would you make many changes?"

"I would refuse to breathe at birth". "But seriously though, I would put more effort into relationships. Three failed marriages don't make me proud. There's much room for improvement".

"Do you ever feel bitter?"

"Never". "Everything is my own responsibility. I've had my

rough times when things have gone wrong but I had only myself to blame. Bitterness does no good, it just eats you up from the inside. We all need to take responsibility for our own actions. It is far too easy to blame others. You have to face yourself, face down your fears, don't run from them, confront them. Take Sarah, she is running away from something, but would she not be far better in facing up to it? Whatever it is, it's not going to go away".

"We don't know what prompted her flight" said Alan. "But maybe by now she's starting to come to terms with it".

"I hope for everyone's sake you're right" said Mike. "When you think about it what are we two old fools doing, you with a chronic disease and me with a problem heart, running around Donegal at the behest of someone we scarcely know, looking for someone we don't know at all? It's madness".

"I didn't know you had heart problems" said Alan.

"I don't say much about it, topic closed".

"Let's find somewhere to spend the night. We can check this woman out in the morning and if it's her, well and good. If not, we head home".

"Agreed" said Mike.

CHAPTER 11

Mike's Tale

Mike's early years are lost in the mists of time. He created many myths and mysteries about his origins. Some of his more impressionable friends believe he is a disinherited peer of the realm, others that he was born into a Belfast docker's family. His accent and speech patterns point to the latter! What is certain is that he joined the army at seventeen and spent most of the rest of his life abroad.

By his mid twenties he was in an elite unit guarding radar stations, a chain of which ran from Northern Sweden to Pakistan which gave NATO its eyes and ears on Russia.

It was in Sweden he met his first wife, in a small village well to the North of Stockholm. She was used to a very quiet life and had no desire to move away from her mother. Tensions developed and, on a week's leave from Pakistan, Mike could bear it no longer. His ultimatum was 'travel with me or it's over'.

His next posting was London and although Ursula tried to settle, the relationship was doomed and she returned to her quiet village where she lived for the rest of her life.

Ironically, it wasn't long after this that Mike decided to leave the army. His last posting had been Munich and he found he liked the Bavarian atmosphere, scenery and people. He was already fluent in Swedish, and picked up German without difficulty. He also picked up some dubious business partners who were smuggling goods into East Germany. He joined with them and increased profits by smuggling people out, as well as goods into, East Germany. Whatever it was he actually did, it certainly made him big sums of money, some of which bought an Irish pub in Munich. He had a very active social life before meeting Ingrid, a striking, statuesque blonde. She refused to marry him, but they were together for almost two years. Then tragedy struck. Ingrid became pregnant but couldn't guarantee the child was Mike's. Always a troubled girl, she couldn't stand the thought of motherhood and her depression became severe. Taking the opportunity of Mike's absence on business, she jumped from a bridge into the river Isar. Mike was distraught. He'd always turned to drink in times of crisis, and this was the greatest tragedy in his life so far.

He was drunk for three months, wouldn't listen to anyone and cut himself off from his friends and business partners. Finally regaining sobriety, he came to his senses to find he was married. His bride was an eighteen year old exotic dancer. Needless to say the marriage didn't last and before long Mike was touring around Munich in his British Racing Green Morgan sports car.

How he managed to keep out of Germany's tax system is a mystery. That he always dealt in cash may provide part of the answer and he had the pub held in the name of his younger brother living in Northern Ireland.

Mike returned regularly to Belfast to see his mother. On such visits he tended to throw the cash around which made many jealous. One night he was set upon when walking back to his mother's. He was badly beaten and spent three days in hospital. To make the point his attackers had not taken his Rolex, nor had they touched his bulging wallet.

A nurse who attended him in hospital was Turkish and knowing he was from Munich, was telling him about the difficulties her brother and his friends faced in trying to get into

Germany to work. In a Catch 22 situation, they could not get into Germany until they had a validated offer of work, but could not get a validated offer of work unless they were resident in Germany. It set Mike thinking and when he returned to Munich, he set about obtaining validated employment offers which he then sold to Turkish emigrants who were prepared to pay huge prices to be able to work in Germany. Surprisingly, it was not deemed illegal.

For Mike, it was a licence to print money. Unfortunately, he was equally good at spending it. Fast cars, fast women and slow racehorses proved to be a disastrous combination.

However, what really ended Mike's European Empire was the fall of communism. When the Berlin Wall came down it ended the smuggling trade to the East and the influx of East Germans looking for work meant there was no longer any demand for Turkish guest workers.

Finances sadly depleted, Mike decided on retirement and chose to return to Northern Ireland opting finally for a seafront apartment in Bangor, looking out over the Marina to the Antrim and Scottish coasts.

He had married yet again before leaving Munich, this time to an Irish girl working in the bar. Once again the relationship failed. There was a variety of reasons. A twenty-five year age difference did not help, especially as the financial fortune which greatly lessened the gap was no longer there. Also, Mike valued his independence and believed in control while not being controlled.

Thus it was as a single man that Mike arrived in Bangor to accept the keys of his apartment.

Although his finances were badly depleted, Mike still had enough to live on and supplemented that with some limited business interests. He had some involvement in massage parlours which, he claimed, were visited by gentlemen seeking a relaxing back and shoulder massage, a cup of tea and some intellectual conversation. He had developed a profitable side line selling replica watches for which there seemed to be a thriving market in the Bangor area. An import/export business covered a multiple of sins which changed regularly.

He was still prone to hit the drink hard at times but generally he was happy with his decision to retire to Bangor, although he did claim that the Ulster climate was bad for his aches and pains of which he had many.

CHAPTER 12

After the difficulties of the previous night Alan and Mike decided to move up market and chose to stay in the Sandlands Hotel and Spa. It was an old, very prestigious hotel dating back in its original form to the 1880s, when passenger steamers brought the well heeled from the Clyde and Liverpool right up to the private pier only a short distance from the hotel.

Standards had slipped from its hey-day. No longer were the gentlemen expected to wear black tie for dinner and piped music had taken the place of the small orchestra, but the present guests still considered themselves a cut above the ordinary, in fact two or three cuts above. This suited the management, because maintaining the image of supremacy enabled them to charge well above the norm, the same high prices keeping the riff-raff from the door.

To be fair the hotel had a lot going for it. Generous European grants had been invested in it over the years to bring it to a standard not usually found in Donegal. The new swimming pool and spa complex was a big draw, as was the 18-hole championship golf course. The hotel had been traditionally a golfing hotel and during the 50s and 60s had been visited by many celebrities. The troubles had put an end to that and although relative peace now existed hotels like the Sandlands had a hard fight to pull pack their position. Golf was no longer enough, there had to be something for everyone, all family members needed to have their needs catered for. Hence the swimming pool, the saunas, steam rooms, jacuzzi, the massage booths, the gym, the tennis courts, the small cinema, children's play area, pool room and squash court. Whatever happened to people making their own entertainment? The food was, by hotel standards, good and the majority of the spacious rooms enjoyed panoramic views of sea and mountain.

It wasn't cheap but it was considered select. As such, Mike felt uncomfortable and saw the hotel as a home for pseuds, and found himself intensely disliking its fakeness. Still, he made up his mind that he would behave himself.

Charles Hendry, the Manager smiled at Mike and Alan as they arrived at reception.

"The girl will be with you in a minute" he said. "Here for the golf?" he enquired, "usually gentlemen together play a few rounds".

"We want two single rooms" announced Mike.

"Of course Sir, as I said the girl will be along in a minute, in the meantime would you like to bring in your luggage?"

"This is it" said Alan, indicating the two battered rucksacks on the floor.

"Very good Sir, but of course when travelling it's better, is it not, to keep one's suits etcetera in the car. But if you want anything steamed or pressed, our facilities are at your disposal. Would you like me to arrange golf for you in the morning? There is a two-ball teeing off at 8.30 am. I know they would be very happy to make it a four- ball. What do you think?"

"I think we'll decide later" said Alan aware that Mike was coming to the explosive stage where he could say or do anything.

"I didn't notice a Polo ground when we arrived" said Mike. "Still it's probably sheltered behind the sand dunes".

"We don't actually have a Polo ground sir".

"Pity" said Mike. With that the receptionist returned to her station.

"Two single rooms? Certainly" she said. "Will you be paying by cheque or credit card?"

"Credit Card".

"That will be a five percent surcharge bringing the total to £230-00".

"What?" said Mike.

"Each" she said.

"That's a bit steep for an out of season stay" said Alan.

"But Sir, included in that is dinner this evening, breakfast tomorrow, a free round of golf and the use of the Spa".

"But no Polo?" said Mike.

The receptionist looked puzzled. "Of course" she said, "it would be cheaper sharing a room".

"We'll pay" said Mike hurriedly.

"Will I get the porter to take your luggage up to your rooms?"

"I think we can manage" said Alan.

"I'm really tired" he said to Mike as they climbed the stairs. "I need to take some of my pills and have a lie down for an hour".

"Sure" said mike. "You come down when you are ready. I'll be in the bar".

Alan lay on the large bed hearing Mike's door close as he headed downstairs. Within a few seconds he was fast asleep.

It was a good hour later when he woke feeling disorientated and very shaky and unstable. He studied himself in the mirror not liking what he saw. The Parkinson's, his chronic friend, as he called it, had been with him now for fourteen years and he was sick, sore and tired of it. It affected everything he did and even changed his body shape as he became more hunched over. His voice, gait, facial expression and balance had all been affected. The only plus point he could think of was that it entitled him to a blue parking card which enabled him to park anywhere. Well almost anywhere, remembering he had been fined for parking too close to a Pedestrian Crossing, for parking at a Bus stop, in a Taxi Rank and on a bend, plus of course, those times when he was legally and correctly parked on double yellow lines but had forgotten to display the blue card! In fact, it was not a very good deal!

He had a quick shower, changed his clothes, well, to be exact, his underwear and socks. Always wear clean knickers his mother had advised. 'You never know when you will be knocked down'. His mother had always been a pessimist!

Refreshed, he made his way downstairs. At the entrance to the bar he froze: the sound was unmistakable, Mike singing the Auld Orange Flute.

Alan stepped quickly over to him. "Not really in character Holmes" he said.

"Sorry Watson, just got a bit carried away"

The residents at the bar looked at him with a mixture of amusement and disgust. They preferred their entertainment to be imported.

"Time to eat" said Alan.

The meal was superb. Alan had French onion soup with a garlic crouton and gruyere cheese, followed by fillet of beef smothered with a Burgundy demi-glace with wild mushrooms, pink peppercorn, garlic and herb butter. He skipped the sweets, finished with coffee and a cheeseboard.

Mike chose a seafood cocktail with lemon sole stuffed with crabmeat and a lobster Bisque for a main course. He finished with hot chocolate fondant.

"They might be a lot of pricks but they can cook" said Mike, none too softly.

Rather embarrassed Alan took a sip of his wine. The house wine was adequate, if overpriced.

"I'll bet the real Sherlock Holmes would have had a better bottle of wine" said Mike.

"He was being paid for his work...remember".

"Don't go petty on me".

Alan gave up. There were times, and this was one of them, when there was just no talking to Mike. For such an intelligent man he could be exceptionally difficult when drinking. However, the evening was well underway and the only thing to do was to try to keep him under control until he decided it was time to sleep.

The Sandlands was a golfing hotel, hence the majority of the guests were golfers who enjoyed the game and the only thing golfers enjoy more than playing the game is talking about it. Hence the conversation in the bar centred on drive lengths, club qualities, birdies at the 7th missed eagle at the 15th, pars at the 13th, the best putter to have and the merits of big-headed drivers.

Although quite a good natural golfer Mike had no real interest in the game. Overall it was a monumental bore to him and after his earlier musical contribution he imagined, probably correctly, that he was being ostracised by those around him. He was drinking heavily and Alan was beginning to wonder if the return to the bar had been such a good idea, when Mike got very unsteadily to his feet and, with a masterpiece of timing, taking advantage of a lull in conversation, enquired very loudly,

"Do any of you fuckers fish?"

Stunned silence.

"No? Well in that case I'm going to bed. Any female under fifty is welcome to join me".

With that he lurched out of the bar colliding with a glass display case which by some miracle remained standing.

"Tired and emotional" Alan announced as he made his way out of the bar leaving behind the stunned clientele.

"You wouldn't believe it" boomed Mike's voice from the top of the stairwell, "not one of those fuckers fish, isn't that amazing".

CHAPTER 13

The next morning told a different tale. Mike took breakfast in his room while Alan walked across the white sand towards the rocks at the end of the bay.

Not for the first time he wondered what he was doing here, on a wild goose chase with a seventy year old who could not be relied upon and could be a positive embarrassment, like last night. They didn't even hold similar values. He supposed it was the old idea of opposites attract, people are attracted to those who can fill in the bits we are missing.

By the time he returned, Mike was up and about, if keeping a low profile.

"Bad night, bad scene" said Mike.

"Put it behind you, we've work to do, let's go and check out this woman".

Alan settled the bill with a stoney faced receptionist. The Manager was nowhere to be seen.

The old Mercedes was pointed North along the narrow road skirting the golf course.

"About five miles I reckon" said Alan.

"I never realised there would be so many caravans" said Mike, "I just assumed there would be a field with caravans in it. All nice and compact, it's like looking for a needle in a haystack".

"I think we'll have to walk the sites" said Alan.

"That'll take a fair time".

"Well it's a beautiful day".

"Better for those without a hangover".

"Self- inflicted, no sympathy".

Their search was shortened when, at the first large site their visit sparked two large Dobermans to life along with the appearance of the site owner with a shotgun cradled in his arms.

"We're closed" he shouted.

"No doubt about it" murmured Mike.

Over an hour later, they were approaching the tip of the peninsula with the old Martello Tower perched on the cliff edge. Here the caravans were more spaced out, often occupying private, secluded sites. Most were completely closed down for winter, with heavy ropes over their roofs to secure them against winter storms with the winds frequently hitting eighty miles per hour.

Carefully packed under the vans was all the paraphernalia of summer fun. Sail boards, canoes, BBQs. , cool boxes, bicycles, everything a family could need.

"What's that?" asked Mike pointing over a small hillock.

"Smoke.... we're in business" said Alan.

They slowly climbed over the little hill and found behind it an elderly, russet coloured caravan with a thin wisp of smoke rising from its stainless steel flu. A youngish looking woman was bending over a radio trying to fit new batteries oblivious to their arrival.

"Reception is very bad here" said Mike.

The woman started perceptively. "Who are you?"

"We're friends of your sister"

"Is she here?"

"No, but she sent us to look for you, are you Sarah?"

"Yes, I am so glad you are here".

Why didn't I expect that, mused Alan.

"We must get to the police" said Sarah.

"We thought you wouldn't be pleased to see us" said Mike.

"Twenty four hours ago that would have been the case, but things have changed".

"Maybe you should explain to us. Oh and I'm Alan and this is Mike".

Sarah talked them through the events of the previous night explaining how the implant functioned and the discussion overheard in the mountain bar. So horrific was the memory of the callous, cold, lack of human concern exhibited that she nearly broke down twice.

"So you see we must get this information to the police" she said finishing.

"Right, let's go" said Mike.

"Hold on a minute" said Sarah. "I've some things to pull together and I must settle up with Mrs Boyce, I'll tell her my uncle has called for me".

"O. K. " said Alan. "Mike can stay here with you while I go to the village to phone Claire and also make sure the police are informed".

The Mercedes headed slowly back along the road with Alan lost in thought. Was her story really true? He couldn't see any reason for making it up yet it was an incredible tale.

The Celtic Tiger years had brought prosperity throughout Ireland, and one sign of this was the number of mobile phones in use, even in places like Donegal where the reception was variable. The downside was that the old pay phones in the public phone boxes had not been updated. The only one in the village had been vandalised, but a note stuck to the door indicated that there was a working public phone at the harbour. Alan got back into the car and drove over to the harbour. As he dialled her number he prayed that Claire would be in. His prayers were answered.

Claire listened to the story without comment.

"I'm speechless" she said when Alan had finished. "Do you think she's in any danger?"

"I shouldn't think so. No one knows anything about her, never mind what she has overheard and we'll be bringing her back with us this afternoon. Now Claire, my change for the phone is running out so I need you to inform the police. Tell them we'll be back this afternoon".

Alan didn't return to the car immediately. Instead, he bought a copy of the Irish Times and took a seat in the small coffee house overlooking the harbour. There were no fishing boats moored. Alan could see that the harbour, on the wrong side of the peninsula, was exposed to winter gales. The small fishing fleet must be moored somewhere else. He thought back to a photo he'd seen of this very harbour, taken about the turn of the 20th century, showing the harbour packed with the herring trawlers and on the quayside dozens of women gutting and salting the herrings and packing them into barrels. Fickle fish though, are herrings, and the great shoals are now long gone. The harbour now only comes alive in the summer as a mooring for holidaymakers' pleasure craft.

The Celtic Tiger had a major impact on the local economy, new houses had sprung up everywhere, although building had outstripped sales, and many were left unfinished or unoccupied. Could be the time to buy, he thought and then caught himself on. What would a 66 year old in his condition want with more property? It would simply be a victory for optimism over reality.

The differences between the photograph, or his memory of it, and the present day were striking and it caused him to think of the improvements to life in Ireland over the century. If truth be told, the greatest changes had come in the last twenty years due to the Celtic Tiger and the peace dividend which had brought a huge increase in the quality of life of the Irish both North and South of the border. It was hard to believe with standards of living already being threatened by the recession, that some extremists would, once again, be prepared to wreck the social and economic fabric of the country in the pursuit of a totally outdated 19th century concept of nationalism.

He opened his paper and began to scan through it as his coffee arrived. His eye caught a headline on an inside page, "Conflict issues new threat". Apparently a new dissident republican group calling itself Coimhlint or Conflict was promising to wage all-out war to win a military victory for Irish Unity. The article indicated that Coimhlint was armed, dangerous and ruthless.

Suddenly Alan had a really bad feeling. He knew he was tense and nervous by the way the Parkinson's was reacting. There was a bit of involuntary movement and a less than steady gait. 'You O. K?" asked the waitress, helping him on with his coat.

"Reasonable" he said, leaving an over- generous tip to speed his departure. He'd only drunk half his coffee but had a feeling that something had gone badly wrong.

He drove quickly back to the caravan, this time driving along the sandy track from the road right up to it.

There was no sign of life. Alan left the car and looked inside. It had been completely trashed. Drawers pulled out, cushions ripped apart, mattress overturned but no sign of Sarah or Mike. He heard a noise outside and peered out to see a very unsteady Mike slowly approach the caravan.

"What the hell happened?" exclaimed Alan.

"I know nothing" said Mike, "I went behind the sand dunes for a pee and the next thing I knew was the sound of your car arriving. By the headache and sore shoulder, I deduce, my dear Watson, that someone slipped up behind me when my defences were down, as it were, and sandbagged me. Imagine doing that to a seventy year old man having a pee. Lucky I have a hard head".

"Are you O. K?" asked Alan, not being familiar with the effects of knocking out a seventy year old.

"I'm fine" said Mike, "just a bit dizzy. As if I didn't have enough trouble with my aches and pains".

"I assume this stems from last night, something must have made them suspicious of her".

"Time for action" said Mike. "First we must let Claire know what has happened, secondly we must try to find Sarah before any harm is done. Time also to see if Mrs Boyce knows anything. We'll have to use her phone. No point in being secretive now".

CHAPTER 14

The two men, suddenly feeling their age, and completely overwhelmed by events, felt their confidence draining. They realised now that they might well be in a life and death situation. Never had they thought they would ever be involved directly with one. They had no experience of, or training in, such matters. The fact that someone's life lay in their hands was a shot of reality greater than either had ever wanted. They looked helplessly at each other and in unison both said "I told you we should not have become involved in this".

"This is no time for recriminations" said Alan, "but we do have to act. At present we're Sarah's only hope".

"Then God help her" muttered Mike.

It was an easy site to run. Most of the caravans belonged to families from the North. Some of them had been coming to Sandhead for over 50 years. Everyone knew and looked out for each other. Mothers looked after stray children on the beach confident that they could rely on the same level of support. Sports equipment and BBQs could be left outside. Theft on the site was unknown, not like some of the neighbouring sites. Mrs Boyce was used to good behaviour, nice people and lawful activities. Off season she normally just locked the gate and closed the site down but for some reason she had taken pity on the young woman who had arrived from out of nowhere. There was something sad and troubled about her that touched Mrs Boyce, and, against all her normal procedures and natural instincts, she agreed to lease her the old caravan which had belonged to the Myles family, and opened the nearby toilet block.

The Myles family had effectively given the caravan to Mrs Boyce when the old man Myles died. He'd been a significant painter in his day and Mrs Boyce had some of the paintings he'd given her on the wall of the hall.

None of the family ever came now, and the thought of a short lease of the caravan appealed to Mrs Boyce. Apart from anything else it would be good for it to be used. She looked out from the kitchen window and saw two strangers approach. One was a heavily built big man, the other a small man with white hair. They both looked unsteady on their feet. She had a premonition of trouble.

"Excuse me" said the smaller man, "are you Mrs Boyce?"

She nodded.

"We're friends of the woman you hired the caravan to. We've been looking for her on behalf of her sister. We found her this morning but now we've lost her again".

"Is she running away from you?"

"No, no, nothing like that, in fact she was very glad to see us, but we are fairly certain that something has happened to her".

Alan took Mrs Boyce through the story to date omitting all the mention of the implant and Sarah's earlier involvement with the Security Services, just saying that she must have been recognised by someone in the bar.

"Kidnapped you think? The poor woman, and you, you poor man, knocked out at your age", Mrs Boyce said to Mike, "let me get you some tea".

"I'm sorry about the caravan" said Alan "It's been well trashed".

"Don't worry about that, there are more serious matters to deal with. First we have to get in touch with the Gardai. Are you quite sure she has disappeared. You didn't actually see anyone?"

"No, but I felt them" said Mike. "It was very convincing".

"The local Gardai are up in the hills supervising the sheep dipping, but I'll ring Letterkenny. They'll be out in half an hour" said Mrs Boyce.

The Gardai officers arrived about forty- five minutes later, looked at the trashed caravan and took statements from Mike and Alan. They then went up to the Mountain bar.

"Something very strange" said the senior Garda officer on their return. "The barman says there was no meeting there last night and furthermore, there was not a single strange female in the bar all night. A young lad playing pool backed up his story".

Mike and Alan looked at each other.

"Are you sure of your facts gentlemen?" asked the Garda Sergeant.

"This young woman didn't want to be tracked down so maybe she trashed the caravan and did a runner after tapping you on the head, sir".

"You see how a different slant can be put on things" said the other Gard.

"We'll record this" said the Sergeant, "but as things stand, we can't assume she's been kidnapped. However, do keep in touch and, if we uncover anything, we'll let you know".

With that they drove off. Mike, Alan and Mrs Boyce looked at each other. The question on all their minds was, "could this be right?"

Alan was the first to speak.

"I don't think she'd be capable of such a thing".

"Neither do I" said Mike.

"I don't know the young woman" said Mrs Boyce, "but I have an idea. There's a man who sometimes works for me. He is a simple soul, not all there, but honest. He lives in a shack up in the hills. He might be simple, but there is not much which goes on in the hills that he doesn't know about. If there was a meeting of strange men in the Mountain bar he'll know about it. That's just the sort of thing the Skunk would pick up on".

"Why is he called the Skunk'?" asked Alan.

"If you ever get near him you'll understand" said Mrs Boyce. "Poor man, it's not his fault, he's been living in the hills for years and has neither in him nor on him. I'm one of the few people he talks to. Most people just make fun of him. I sometimes give him a meal and some of my dead husband's old clothes. I'll go up into the hills and see if I can find him. In the meantime you can try to put the caravan back together".

The two men walked slowly back to the caravan, wondering if their intervention had not just made things worse, and generally feeling sorry for themselves. It was with little enthusiasm, and even less skill, that they attempted to restore the caravan to a semblance of normality.

It was a good two hours before Mrs Boyce returned.

"Well" she said, "I knew the Skunk would know. He told me he saw a number of men going into the Mountain Bar, only one of whom was local and him a really bad boy".

"Has he any idea where the men might have taken the woman?" asked Alan.

"He wasn't very clear, I don't think he saw the woman. He is very shy of young women, especially since he was accused of assault on one fifteen years ago. Of course he was innocent, but it made him even more of a recluse. He was going on about Pinnacle Rock but that's just above Mary's Bay and there's nothing there, no houses, no caravans, no buildings. Wait a moment though, there used to be an old barn up there. I don't even know if it's still there. I haven't been up there for years".

"Mrs Boyce, that's been a great help and of course we'll pay for the damage done to the caravan" said Alan, conscious that she was looking round disdainfully.

"I suppose I can tidy up when you leave".

After Mrs Boyce left Holmes and Watson looked at each other. Neither spoke. Mike spoke first, "We have to find her".

"I'm afraid I agree with you," said Alan, "even though every instinct in my body is screaming run! They must be holding her in that old barn Mrs Boyce spoke of. I've a vague idea where it might be. I think we've no option but to go and try to rescue her and we'll have to do it tonight".

Claire had been really alarmed after Mike had given her an update and decided to contact Commander Harris. She got right through to him on his private number. She had met Harris in the company of Inspector Linton and Sergeant Smyth. Harris was an attractive looking man recovering from his second divorce. He wasn't sure why he had given Claire his personal number.

CHAPTER 15

"Jesus Christ",he repeated, almost in anguish. The others fell silent and looked at him expectantly.

"I knew I'd seen her before, she's security".

"Who are we talking about?" asked Joe.

"The woman in the bar, sitting in the shadows beside the door. I saw her when Mick turned up the lights to clear the bar. I knew I recognised her but just couldn't place her. It's been bugging me, but now I have her. It would've been six years ago in London, remember the time when we were trying to do a deal with the Syrians. She was associated with a Lebanese women's group and, if my memory serves me well I think her cover had just been blown and she'd been stood down. They must've returned her to active service".

"Now hold on a minute" said a somewhat elderly, kindly, grandfatherly figure, "we don't know if it is this woman, if she is still working for MI5, if she was here by accident or design and if she heard anything".

"What happens if she turns out to be all of those things?" asked Joe.

"Why, you kill her" said the kindly grandfather. "We can't risk Conflicts operations being compromised".

"First thing is to find her. Mick will know" said Francis.

Mick was dozing on a chair by the door. "Going so early?"he said sarcastically.

"No lip" said Joe. "Who was the girl in here on her own earlier?"

"Never saw her before, why, do you fancy her?"

"We need to talk to her" said the grandfather figure appearing in the bar.

"Of course Mr Devlin" said Mick, struggling to his feet. "I don't know her, but some of the young people in last night will know her. I'll find out as soon as I can. By the way, I thought it a bit strange when I suggested a better seat in the light, she opted to remain where she was. Would you like a round of drinks or perhaps somewhere to kip for an hour?"

"We can rest after we get the girl" said Francis, "but an early breakfast wouldn't go amiss".

The news filtered in. The woman was called Rose Blaney, she had a caravan at Sandhead, she was alone, had no visitors, kept herself to herself, had no car and never made phone calls.

"Right" said Francis, "if she's still there we can pick her up. She won't have had time to talk to anyone, and she must have a tape recorder of some type, because evidence of memory without the actual transcripts, would be treated as hearsay. So find her and find the recorder".

The two watchers from the hill watched the elderly Merc leave the site. One spoke into an RT.

"A couple of old boys, could be relatives, no threat. One has just left but the other is still here".

"We'll come down now. Neutralise the old boy. Tap him on the head and give him a whiff of ether to keep him out but do not kill him. Over and out".

Sarah's first thought as she saw Francis was "Oh, he came to find me" but then reality set in as she noted the four men with him, all from last night's meeting. "Shit," she thought, "We're in trouble". However, her old security training returned and she appeared calm and collected.

"Can I help you?" she said. "If it's a caravan you want it's Mrs

Boyce you need to speak to".

"We need to talk to you" said Francis, "why are you here?"

"Just spending some time by myself, get out of the rat race for a time, a holiday, what business is it of yours anyway?"

"You are Rose Blaney?"

"Yes"

"Well Rose, we need to find your tape recorder, you know, the little mini recorder you use".

"I don't know what you mean. I don't have a recorder".

"But I remember you had one in London six years ago". He could see she was thrown off balance.

"Now Rose you can save a lot of time if you simply produce it. You see we want to know if you overheard any conversation in the bar last night".

"I didn't, I don't listen to people's conversations. Why should I be the slightest bit interested in what you were talking about"?

Francis smiled. "Now Rose".

"She is not Rose," called a voice from inside the van. " She's Sarah Scott" said the younger of the watchers brandishing an Irish passport.

Francis tutted. "Really Rose, I mean Sarah, if you tell lies about your name, what else would you lie about?"

"Have you found it yet?" he shouted into the caravan.

"No sign".

"Sarah, I'm afraid as they say in the best police dramas.... You will have to come with us to help with our enquiries".

"What about my uncle?"

"He is sleeping peacefully behind the sand dunes" said the other watcher.

"O.K. Let's go" said Francis. "Bind her, blindfold her and carry her".

CHAPTER 16

Commander Harris reacted quickly to Claire's phone call and a video conference was set up with the Gardai Siochana.

"So it's now kidnapping by person or persons unknown" said Garda Deputy Commissioner Burke.

"Yes we think now that there's much more to it. We feel she may inadvertently have stumbled upon something like a dissident cell" explained Harris.

"Oh, I don't think that is very likely in Donegal" said Burke defensively. "What do you think Halford?"

Halford nodded and explained that criminal and terrorist offences were at an all time low in Donegal and if there were any dubious goings on, he would know about them. However, he promised to review the situation, and he and Deputy Commissioner Burke pledged to do everything they could to help.

Burns had said little during the video conference but, as they were leaving, he moved over to speak to Harris. "I hope you don't mind but I'm taking a couple of days leave" he said.

"What, in the middle of this, leaving me to it?"

"I just felt a break would do me good".

"Just wonderful, what timing" said Harris. "Where are you planning to go anyway?"

"I thought a couple of days in Donegal might be nice?"

"Ahh...take care" said Harris knowingly.

Six hours later, Burns registered at the Sandlands Hotel complete with golf clubs and Pringle sweater.

"Business or pleasure?" enquired the receptionist.

"Oh very much pleasure" was the reply.

Sarah had been blindfolded for the journey and was literally carried to her place of confinement. It was a small dark windowless room.

"Now, things can be easy or hard, it's for you to decide" said Francis.

"Why are you in Donegal?"

"For a rest".

"Since when have you been working again for MI5?"

"I'm not".

"Who were the two men with you?"

"My uncle and his friend".

"Why were you in the pub last night?"

"For a drink".

"Why did you choose to sit in shadows beside the door?"

"I'm a shy woman".

"Did you hear any of the discussions from the next room?"

"No I don't listen to private conversations".

"Where is your recorder?"

"I don't have one".

"Are you wired for sound at the minute?"

"No".

"Search her".

"Take off your clothes please".

She did as she was asked and, when naked, did a little playful pirouette.

"Bend over", a painful, brutish internal examination followed.

"Put your pants and bra back on". "Now again, how long have you been working for MI5?"

"I'm not".

"Who gave you the background information on us?"

"No-one".

"Who told you there was a meeting arranged for last night?"

"I didn't know there was a meeting".

"I've had enough of this", said the grandfatherly Mr Devlin, stepping forward and drawing the back of his hand across her face, cutting her with the diamond ring he wore. Sarah felt the taste of blood in her mouth. A second blow loosened a tooth whilst a third blow to the body, she was certain, had cracked a rib. She knew she was lucky, because the windowless room was too small to enable them to get a real swing to put force behind the blows.

"I'm afraid we'll have to leave you briefly" said Francis, "food's ready, of course you aren't getting any, but I'll leave you with a parting thought. They say the big toe on a human's foot is essential to maintain balance" he paused, "and so easy to remove" he said, indicating the bolt cutters beside the wall.

When he'd left, Sarah tried her bonds but they were tight. Escape wasn't an immediate option. She looked around the little room. There was something strange yet familiar about it. Suddenly the penny dropped, she realised where she was.

Dusk came, and the old Mercedes shook and juddered down a very rough lane. "The car's behaving the way I feel" said Alan. About half a mile further on, the track petered out. "I can't see where we are going, we'll have to leave the car here" said Alan.

They climbed out, totally ill equipped for the conditions. Trainers, jeans, loose sweatshirts and light waterproof jackets were not ideal for the time of year. They could just make out the rough outline of the barn ahead, looking completely deserted, which greatly boosted their morale. In reality, each was scared stiff but too proud to admit it to each other.

"There seems to be a fence around it" said Mike.

"Any ground cover ahead?" asked Alan. He didn't know what it meant but he'd heard it used in reports from Afghanistan and it sounded good.

"Plenty" replied Mike, "Shit".

"What's wrong".

"Nothing, it's shit that I'm standing in".

"It's good luck".

"Not for you if my shoes are all shitty when we get back to your car".

"You'll just have to take them off then, or travel in the boot".

This gentle banter could go on for ages but they realised they were simply postponing the evil hour. They crept silently towards the barn, well fairly silently, or at least as silently as two geriatrics could wheeze and stumble.

"Get down" said Alan, dropping to his knees into something warm and sticky which he was sure wasn't a toffee pudding.

"What can you see?" whispered Mike, "God you smell like the Skunk".

"They've left a guard, look over by the side of the barn". A distinctive figure could just be made out standing in the shadows, close to the barn door.

"Since I was the one knocked out, I should be the one to tap that gentleman on the head" announced Mike.

"O. K. " said Alan, almost too rapidly, "after all you didn't get to hit the AA man".

"Right" whispered Mike, "no-more talking, let's get over the fence".

He mounted the fence which collapsed under his weight.

"Bloody idiot" hissed Alan, putting one arm over the fence to vault over. Suddenly he found himself suspended by three strands of barbed wire, three feet off the ground.

"Mike, you'll have to free me" he whispered.

"Think I have broken my fuckin' ankle" said Mike.

"Never mind that" said a panicking Alan. Mike hobbled over. "I can't free this" he said, "I'll have to cut the jacket off", which he did with some gusto.

"Don't worry" he said, "it looked cheap and nasty"

"Yeah, it was yours, I borrowed it last year and forgot to give it back".

"To business then. I'll circle around from behind" said Mike. "If he sees me before I hit him, charge him from the front".

"Right", said Alan, more to keep Mike's morale high, than with any intention of obeying the order.

The strategy went extremely well. Having circled round from behind the barn only colliding once, with an abandoned feeding trough, it was with surprising agility that Mike spun around the corner and struck the figure a tremendous blow to the side of the head with a piece of wood taken from the broken fence.

"Well done" said Alan running to join him.

"I did it. I did it" whispered Mike.

"You certainly did" said Alan looking at the collapsed scarecrow.

"Let's hope she's inside" said Mike. But of course nothing was inside the barn, nor had been for some time.

On the journey back to the car, tired and disappointed, they encountered two sheep dogs.

"Always liked dogs" said Mike, "I have a way with them".

"Well this is the time to use it" said Alan, as the dogs stood in front of them, snarling with teeth bared.

"Down boy, fuck off will you". The dogs refused to let them pass. Try as they might the two men couldn't get past the snarling dogs. They then moved to the left and to their surprise, the dogs let them, walking slowly alongside.

"We are being herded like sheep" said Alan.

"Bloody well smell like sheep!" was Mike's comment.

"Of course" said Alan, "they think we're some large breed of sheep and they're taking us to....."

"What's that ahead?"interrupted Mike.

"It's the sheep dip".

"That I draw the line at. I'm not going to be driven through the sheep dip by a couple of stupid dogs who can't tell the difference between a man and a sheep" said Mike.

The dogs approached from behind starting to snap their ankles.

"I wish I'd held on to that piece of wood" said Mike,"I fucking well refuse to be driven through a sheep dip by a couple of dogs, but I reserve the right to walk through myself" he added quickly, wading waist deep through a channel of chemicalised water. Alan did the same. The dogs looked as if they were laughing.

"What a mess the car will be in".

"What a mess you are in" said Mrs Boyce half an hour later. "Let's get you cleaned up".

Cleaned up and wearing some clothes of the late Mr Boyce, too big for Alan and too small for Mike, they sipped hot whiskeys and started to feel slightly better.

"I was talking to the Skunk again" said Mrs Boyce. "He's a bit simple and hard to follow at times, but when he was talking about Pinnacle Rock, he was really thinking of Mary's Bay, below the rock and was talking about a boat, a large, newly arrived fishing boat now moored there".

"We'll look into it in the morning" said Alan, the waves of exhaustion breaking over him, "we'll sleep in the caravan tonight if that's alright" he said turning to Mrs Boyce.

"Certainly" she said, "now explain to me again about the dogs and the sheep dip".

Back at the caravan both men were so tired they could only manage one large whiskey as a nightcap before falling asleep amidst the debris of the caravan, with the pungent smell of sheep dip in every pore. 'I wonder, does it protect against swine flu?' thought Alan as he dozed off!

Both men woke with a start. A tall, well built, young man stood over them.

"Unusual taste in aftershave gentlemen" he said. "my name is Burns, I act as liaison between PSNI and MI5".

"What are you doing here?" asked Mike.

"I'm on holiday, but thought I might be able to give you a hand with your search for Sarah. I'm assuming you haven't already rescued the damsel in distress?"

"No but we now know where she's being held" said Alan proudly.

"Do share the information".

"Hold on a minute" said Mike, "How do we know who, or what you are?"

Burns flipped his identification card and looked enquiringly at the two men.

"Well, let's hear it then".

"She's on a boat in Mary's Bay".

"Is she now?" said Burns thoughtfully, "I bet the boat will be the Juno, which we've been keeping a close eye on recently. We've good reason to believe that she acts as a mobile headquarters and bomb factory for Coimhlint or Conflict. It's a dissident republican splinter group promising to unite Ireland by force. It's a very violent and brutal organisation. The Juno arrived here two days ago, bringing the Southern leadership to meet with their Northern counterparts. I'm afraid Sarah picked the wrong time for her little excursion. It's essential that we retrieve her and the equipment installed in her".

"You make her sound like a robot" said Mike.

"I'm sorry to appear unfeeling but I must make things clear. We need that information and to get it we need her body, dead or alive".

Mike and Alan paled as they looked at each other.

"How can we rescue her?" asked Mike.

"That depends on whether or not she has talked. If she has, she'll be dead by now and the equipment cut out and destroyed. If she hasn't talked, we might be able to rescue her but we'll have to act quickly before they break her".

"If only we could send her a message to hold on".

"Of course, why didn't I think of that, just wait for the bloody postman" said Burns sarcastically, betraying his inner tensions. He felt a degree of guilt about Sarah since it was his thoughtless approach which had caused her to run in the first place. He put it to the back of his mind. Personal feelings, and the type of work he did, just did not sit easily side by side.

"We can't do anything until this evening" he said, "but we must make plans. Come and have lunch with me and we can discuss strategy".

Both men nodded.

"Where and when?" asked Alan.

"My hotel, one o'clock".

"Which is your hotel?" asked Mike

"Sandlands"

"I thought it might be".

On board the Juno Sarah was feeling anything but happy. 'Who would ever think I was being held on a boat?'. She reviewed her position. She was being held captive by a violent terrorist organisation whose members suspected her of spying and who wouldn't hesitate to take her life. On the plus side, two geriatric friends of her sister were looking for her, aided by positive thoughts from Claire. Not good odds she thought. Whether or not the Gardai, PSNI or MI5 were involved, she didn't know. She was on her own and she realised her only hope was to bluff her way out of it, so she steeled herself for the ordeal to come. If she fainted it might buy some time. If she could convince them that she was ill they might bring her up on deck which would increase the chances of escape. In one way she was relieved to realise she was on board a boat, for it explained the unsteady unbalanced feeling she had which she'd feared marked the return of the vertigo she'd experienced some years earlier. This gave her confidence and she was now prepared to play the role of her life.

Francis returned. "Please tell me how you recorded the information" he asked, glancing meaningfully at the bolt cutters.

Lunch was a quiet affair. Mike kept a very low profile but couldn't avoid the Manager who viewed his unkempt attire with disdain.

"Been looking after your Polo ponies sir?" he asked.

"What was that about? You don't look like a Polo man to me" said Burns.

"Long story" said Mike, "a bit of a misunderstanding. Let's take our coffee in the lounge and you can explain to us what your plan is".

They moved across into the lounge area, very expensively furnished and with paintings of local scenes by renowned artists adorning the walls. Each, Mike noticed, carried a 5 figure price tag. He wondered just how many people coming on a golfing holiday went home with a £10,000 painting in the boot of the car.

"Now listen to me" said Burns, when the coffee had been poured, "we'll only have one chance at this end and we need a team of three, fit, trained men to make the plan work. Of course we don't have them, all we have is you, can either of you row?"

"I can" said Mike, "I used to row a lot when I lived in Sweden, or do I mean I rowed a lot with the wife! Probably both".

"Cut the funnies" said Burns, - "this is serious". Turning to Alan, he asked "Ever set a detonator?"

"No"

"Time to learn".

"Now" he said, "this is the plan. Conflict has a very small arms storage facility on the upper shores of Mary's Bay. It was an old dump, originally one of the PIRAs but it only had a thin coating of concrete to seal it at decommissioning time. Conflict knew where it was and took it over. No one was particularly worried because the weapons were antiquated and the explosives low quality.

"The Juno's a different kettle of fish. She may look like a fishing boat but she's very fast and well equipped. She serves as a mobile HQ for Conflict but she's also a deadly bomb- making factory. There's a special container on deck which can be moved about or lifted off. It's a completely self-contained little bomb factory with its own washing facilities, so that no traces of explosives can be transferred to the Juno. I know, we've raided her twice and both times she was as clean as a whistle and of course, no sign of the container.

"Someone knew we were coming. Juno has a small crane on board and we believe the bomb making facility can be lowered to the seabed when completely sealed without fear of damage to contents. All this makes it very difficult to get evidence. She was boarded by the Fishery Protection people last month, but no fish and no container were evident. The people on board said they were on a pleasure trip.

"Our plan is simple. There are eight Conflict Leaders here plus a few foot soldiers. Two, possibly three, of the Northern Leaders are already on their way home. That leaves five on the boat.

"Tonight Alan, you'll set detonators which I'll give to you, at or around the location of the arms dump I'll show you this afternoon.

"Mike, you will row me out to the Juno. When the detonators go off at least some of the men on board will come ashore to investigate. Mike will help me board the Juno. I'll deal with the two or possibly three men on board. I'll release Sarah and Mike will row us to the shore where Alan will be waiting. I'll try to ensure a Garda presence on the shore, but I can't guarantee it"

"Two problems"said Alan. "One, the Juno's tender has an engine so it can cut you off from the shore, and two, assuming you get to the shore what happens then? Do they just sit, look and wave bye, bye?"

"Well", said Burns, "Mike'll have to row very bloody quickly and you'll have to have the getaway car standing ready".

CHAPTER 17

It was one of those black, wet nights with a small moon frequently obscured by scudding clouds.

"I wish you hadn't cut the jacket to ribbons" said Alan.

"Sure didn't Mrs Boyce get you an old coat".

"It itches".

"Poor man with sensitive skin", mocked Mike. "Let's go and meet Mr Burns".

"I'm really not up to this" said Alan shaking visibly.

"You'll be fine never fear, don't think about it".

They met Burns as arranged on the North shore of Mary's Bay.

"Man you look the part" said Mike, viewing Burns through the mist. Dressed all in black, he could have made a Milk Tray advertisement there and then.

Burns took Alan along the shore to what appeared to be a sunken slipway running down from what had once been a small boat house.

"They surely don't store arms here", said Alan.

"No, no they're in a specially built underground cistern. We have our sources", he said, noting the surprise on Alan's face.

"You expect me to set detonators off here. Sure the whole bloody place could go up and me with it. It's about as safe as looking for a gas leak with a match".

"It's quite safe, the detonators would have to be beside the explosives before there was any danger. Now you know the signal, when Mike gets me close to the Juno, I'll flash the torch and you can start the fireworks".

Burns left Alan to his own devices and headed back through the darkness to where he had left Mike, only Mike was not there! From further down the beach he heard a voice and the noise of static. Thank God it was a black night.

"Come in Juno. Come in Juno". Another burst of static.

"Juno I've picked up one of the old boys, actually it was the one I tapped at the caravan. He says he's alone and I don't see signs of anyone else".

Because of the static Burns couldn't hear the reply from Juno. However, within minutes Juno's tender arrived and Mike was bundled in. The tender headed back to the Juno.

Burns cursed his luck. He noted one man in the tender was one he thought had left. The odds worsened. Burns made his way back to the old boathouse.

"Shit, you scared me" said Alan. "Why aren't you on your way out to Juno?"

"Change of plan, your friend's been captured. Now you'll have to row me out and we'll tie one of these rubber dingys to the rowboat. Out at Juno I'll stay in the dingy until you get back to shore and start the fun and games. When the tender from Juno arrives you must disable the engine to slow up whatever action they may take. "

On the Juno, the Council of Coimhlint sat round the table. "Maybe she's telling the truth" said one.

"Security people can't tell the truth because they don't understand the concept", said Francis.

Below the cabin in the small dark room Sarah sat on the edge of a stool and viewed her bandaged foot. They hadn't taken the big toe, instead they'd removed the small toe from her right foot. The pain had been intolerable and if it hadn't been for the rag stuffed in her mouth she would've screamed the place down. At least they'd allowed her to wash her foot and bandage it as best she could. At last the blood had stopped flowing. She was still in a state of shock and could hardly think clearly. The pain was so severe she would've thrown herself off a tall building had there been one handy. Still, she'd stuck to her story and had given nothing away.

Meanwhile, out in Mary's Bay, a small rowing boat towing an inflatable dingy was making its erratic way through the darkness to the Juno. Progress was somewhat erratic because the Parkinson's affected Alan's left side more than the right. Hence with his left arm significantly weaker than his right there was the real danger of rowing in a large circle.

Mike was furious as he was pushed up the ladder onto the Juno.

"What the fuck is this?"he blustered. "Standing minding my own business when this young skitter jumps me?"

"At least you weren't having a pee this time".

"So it was you. I'll remember that in future".

"You don't have a future old man".

"Lock him in downstairs with the woman. We can feed both of them to the fish later".

"I'll have you know that I hold a Swedish passport" said Mike. "I'm a Swedish citizen. This could produce an international incident".

"Some chance" said Joe. "Take him below".

When the door was closed and locked, Mike whispered to Sarah "Did you tell them anything"?

"Nothing".

"How have they treated you so far?"

"Well, they've only cut off one toe".

"You're joking".

"Listen, these people were involved in the Omagh bomb. If they could do that they could do anything. Have you brought help with you?"

Mike quickly and simply explained the plan to her although stressing that now he'd been captured, it was subject to change. Just with that three explosions shook the air.

In the cabin above, the conversation ceased for a moment and a look of puzzled concern crossed the faces of those at the table.

"It sounded as if it came from the arms dump" said Francis, "Joe, take two or three with you in the tender and see what's happened".

As the four men left in the tender, Burns climbed on board by way of the anchor chain. He'd sussed out the best way to the cabin where the prisoners were being held, and quickly made his way down, unlocked the door and stepped inside.

"Thank God" said Sarah.

"Thank us" said Mike, "God was a bit busy when we asked for divine intervention".

Burns quickly cut their bindings and they crept up on deck.

"I'll go and bring the dingy around" said Burns, "You," looking at Sarah, "wouldn't make it down the anchor chain with your foot and you" looking at Mike, "could just never make it. Hide in the shadows and I'll bring the dingy round to the ladder", he said, slipping down the anchor chain. Within minutes he was by the ship's side climbing quickly up the ladder.

"You're very welcome, join the party" said Mike's captor pointing a small black pistol directly at Burn's forehead as he came up the ladder to deck level.

At that moment Mike emerged from the shadows with a club he had unearthed from somewhere, and landed a blow which nearly took the man's head off.

"Down the ladder quickly" said Burns.

The grandfatherly Mr Devlin stepped out of the wheelhouse.

"What's going on?" he shouted. "Mick where are you?"

Paddling very quickly is not a silent exercise, and as three paddles struck the water, nothing could disguise the splashes.

On shore, the men realised something was amiss and ran back to the tender. But in spite of repeated attempts, its engine wouldn't start. In the darkness they didn't notice that the fuel line had been disconnected.

"Row" said Joe.

"Paddle like fuck" shouted Mike as the powerful twin engines of the Juno fired into life, and two powerful searchlights played on the water.

"We're sitting ducks" said Mike.

"They haven't seen us yet" replied Burns. "They're going to pick up the men in the tender first, but that will only take a minute. I wonder where I left those spare detonators?"

Suddenly an incredible noise rent the air. It was like a magnified W.W.2 siren, which is exactly what it was. It certainly distracted the crew of the Juno. One of the search lights directed its beam to the old boathouse, picking up the figure of Alan turning a handle with his right hand and violently shaking some piece of equipment with his left. The second searchlight also focused on the boathouse and a couple of shots rang out, bullets striking just above Alan's head.

"That has bought us some time, I hope he's alright" said Burns "but we're not home yet" as the search lights picked them out. The noise of Juno's twin diesels increased as she got her bearings "They're trying to run us down" cried Sarah.

Just as the awful reality began to sink in, the horizon behind the bay shore began to brighten and over the hill with all lights blazing, appeared two Garda cars, three army land rovers and three armoured personnel carriers.

The Juno crew, now less confident in shallow water, reduced speed and, for a moment, looked at a loss. Then weighing up the odds, they executed a quick turn and headed seawards at top speed.

Burns and Mike paddled the dingy to shore where they were greeted by Halford wearing combat fatigues.

"You arrived in the nick of time" said Burns.

"We did cut it a bit fine, but we never expected you'd do the rescue on your own".

"Not exactly on his own" muttered Mike.

Into the glare of the arc lights erected by the army came Alan.

"What the hell were you doing with that siren affair?"

"I found it and thought it'd be a good idea to create a diversion and also bring out witnesses to what was happening", replied Alan, looking over at the growing crowds of locals gathering behind the police lines.

"It certainly distracted them" said Burns, "and it was a magnificent backdrop to the arrival of the 7th cavalry, but what were you shaking?"

"Well I found the old siren, it must've dated back to the Emergency, (how the South described their time during W. W. 2" he said to Mike.)"However the turbo modulator wasn't working and the only way to operate it at peak volume was to rhythmically shake it up and down. So I thought, shaking is one thing I can do well, so away we went. It worked well didn't it!"

"Certainly did" said Mike. "I was bit worried when they started shooting at you".

"You were worried, I was scared stiff".

"How are you?" Halford asked Sarah.

"Tired, scared, cold and hungry", came the reply.

"We need to get that foot looked at" said Mike. Burns lifted and carried her to an ambulance which had just arrived.

"What time is it?" asked Alan.

"Five thirty am".

"We should give Claire a ring to let her know Sarah is safe".

"She's on her way with Commander Harris", said Burns.

"They should be here in a couple of hours".

In the distance a loud explosion was heard and the western sky briefly lit up.

"Ah, I remember now where I left those detonators" said Burns.

"Dangerous business making bombs in a boat".

"Yes indeed" said Halford. "very unusual for an ordinary fishing boat to blow up".

"I suppose Conflict will try to park the blame with MI5" said Burns.

"Difficult" said Halford, "since no one from MI5 was here".

"Thank you" said Burns.

He walked briskly over to the ambulance.

"I'm sorry, Sarah, for the way I approached you initially. It was totally crass and out of order. I really thought that you'd be happy to be active again".

"Well I wouldn't, not then, not now, not ever".

"We'll arrange to have the devices removed. A London surgeon on our books will fly over and perform the surgery in the Ulster Clinic".

"I suppose you did save my life, although you did put it in danger in the first place".

"I know, I really am sorry. As a poor recompense can I buy you dinner when your foot heals?"

"I'll think about it".

Commander Harris and Claire made good time on their journey and arrived just as dawn was breaking.

"Good job, well done" said Harris to Burns. "Please relay our thanks to Deputy Commissioner Burke" he said to Halford. He then walked over to where Alan and Mike were standing.

"Well gentlemen, you've been in the thick of things".

"The old horse for the hard road" said Mike.

"If you don't mind me saying so neither of you look very steady" said Harris. "I think you should maybe go into Letterkenny for a quick check- up".

"Oh I don't think we'll be doing that" said Alan, "but before we do anything we must go back and speak to Mrs Boyce. She's been very good to us and we've brought her nothing but trouble. We'll have to pay for the damage to the caravan".

"I think we'll be able to look after that" said Halford.

"Looks like a nice place for a holiday" said Harris, "beautiful scenery, wonderful beaches, mountains, it has it all. Can't understand why I've never been here before. "

"I would like to meet Mrs Boyce" said Claire coming over from where the ambulance, taking Sarah to the hospital, had just left.

"I'll come too" said Harris. "We'll take your car and leave mine here", he said opening the door. "God, what is that stink, smells like sheep shite"

"Close" said Alan "but it's a long story, maybe we should take your car instead".

"Well I never, well I never. What a tale. Sure you wouldn't see better on the television and Rose, I mean Sarah, poor soul, losing a toe like that".

They were comfortably seated in Mrs Boyce's kitchen. She had insisted on making bacon, eggs and toast for them and only when they started to eat did they realise how hungry they were. Mrs Boyce had listened avidly to the details and could not wait to tell her friend, Mrs Fegan, but was far too well mannered to rush her guests away. Eventually Alan got to his feet, "Is there any way we could thank the Skunk?" he asked, "his information was really valuable to us"

"You know, he doesn't have a colour television, just an old black and white set".

"I'll leave you a cheque for a new T. V. and a man called Halford who works for the Southern Government, will look after the caravan repairs. We'll be taking Sarah's things back with us and, once again many thanks for all your help".

"I hope I'll see you and your sister again" said Mrs Boyce, speaking to Claire. "I trust her experience hasn't put her off Donegal. She seemed to really like it before all this happened.

"What a really lovely old lady" said Claire, as they walked back to the car.

"When Sarah is feeling up to it we must come over and see her".

CHAPTER 18

A gigantic explosion rent the air and the Juno lifted on a tidal wave.

"Bloody good job you had the sense to get rid of the container factory" said Francis to Mr Devlin.

"I just knew your man would try something" said Devlin. "Joe and I discussed it, sure if I'd been wrong we could've retrieved it later".

"Where to now?" asked Sean, "sure they'll be looking for us North and South".

"They'll assume the blast finished us off" said Devlin. "That should buy us a few days, mind you, the loss of the container has dealt a savage blow to our plans, but we need to strike back quickly to show we're still in business".

Dawn had broken as they cut their way through the Atlantic swell. The Juno was by no means a small boat but one minute she appeared to be at the bottom of a trough with massive dark sea walls on either side, the next it was like sitting at the top of a roller coaster run, perched high on top of the swell with everything lying forty or fifty feet below.

"I suppose fishermen never think of the dangers or get fearful of the power of the sea" said Joe.

"It's their job, they are born to it" said Devlin, "now first thing we need to do is to make a few alterations to Juno to make her less recognisable. There's a secluded bay at the back of Tory which should hide us from prying eyes for a week or more".

The sun was now well up and Tory stood out clearly in the distance. At this time of year there would be few, if any, visitors on the Island, and the islanders themselves would pay no attention to Juno or her crew.

The loss of the container bomb factory was a big loss to Coimhlint both in operational and prestige terms. As a splinter group and one not supporting the Good Friday Agreement they did not have much support in their own community never mind the general populace, but they had intended to rely on the flair and ingenuity of a short, but brutal campaign to blast themselves to the forefront of the negotiating table, outshining the much longer established and more powerful republican brother organisations. "We'll put them in the shade" boasted Devlin, "Coimhlint will preside over the new dawn of an Ireland united by our efforts with a clear timetable for Brit withdrawal".

During their stay on Tory, the Juno had been significantly altered. The green hull was now dark blue and plywood structures ensured she presented a different profile. Juno was painted out to be replaced by Amethyst and the deck and wheelhouse roof were repainted in red to confuse any aerial sightings.

Some of the Coimhlint leaders had decided to leave after a few days, taking a motor boat to the Donegal coast and thereafter a local supporter's car to Letterkenny, where they were stopped and arrested at one of the many roadblocks set up on Halford's instructions.

Mr Devlin, Sean, Joe and Francis, comprising some of the most senior leaders decided to stay on board and see what alternate plan they could devise.

They realised they needed a high profile target, a major propaganda coup to re-establish their credibility. Certainly if it got out that they were bested in Donegal by two elderly, chronically ill gentlemen, helped by a 40 year old woman, they would never again have any credibility in republican circles.

It was Francis who came up with the idea. "What" he asked, "is Belfast most famous for?"

"Linen, tobacco, rope works" said Sean.

"Ship building" suggested Joe.

"Close" said Francis, "The Titanic".

"I have news for you son" said Mr Devlin, "It was sunk by an iceberg in 1912 and it wasn't even a republican iceberg!"

"But preparations to mark the 100th anniversary are already making headlines and it will all focus on the new Titanic centre which is nearly complete, and sits conveniently for us on the bank of the River Lagan. Can you imagine the worldwide publicity such a hit would generate?"

"But we lost most of our explosives when the factory container blew up" said Joe.

"Now I like this idea, and I think I know where we may be able to get a small amount of high quality explosive" said Mr Devlin, "but it'll take some time. I reckon we are safe enough here until it can be delivered".

"In the meantime, we can do nothing so it gives us an opportunity to practice our Irish and deepen our knowledge of Irish culture, including an appreciation of the Tory Primitive School of painting".

"I used to paint like that when I was at school" said Sean.

"I'm going to spend some time walking the island" said Francis, "you never know, we might soon be short of fresh air".

The arrest of the two Coimhlint leaders in Letterkenny was reported by all the media outlets but on the 'Amethyst' they took the news, that two of their team had been picked up, surprisingly calmly.

"If they stick to what we agreed things should be alright" said

Devlin – "they were never on Juno and haven't heard from us since they left Donegal, so there's nothing to make us feel anxious".

"I wouldn't be so certain" said Joe. "Look at this".

Coming into view was a grey Irish Naval vessel.

"It's a fishery protection vessel. We don't want them on board" said Francis. "Take me over in the tender to meet them. I'll say we are German visitors on a tour round Ireland and have decided to spend a few days on Tory".

"Will they not wonder why we haven't moored in the harbour?"

"Birdwatching" said Francis, "we are viewing the birds on the cliffs".

Mr Devlin watched as Francis climbed on board 'Maeve' the fishery protection vessel. "Hope they don't check us out on their computer".

"Shouldn't be a problem, small boats like us don't have to register on the Database, it's up to the owner, so if he doesn't turn up the 'Amethyst' on the database, no one will consider it strange".

"I think that went O. K. " said Francis on his return. "But they did ask if we came across the Juno or any flotsam which may have appeared strange".

The package they were waiting for arrived a day, later looking and feeling, like loaves of bread.

"We have an invitation to dine with the King of Tory before leaving" said Devlin.

The dinner went well, the visitors judging it wise to limit their alcohol intake and to buy three of the King's paintings.

"Derek Hill said I was the best" he proudly announced, "you'll find them increasing in value, a good investment against inflation and valuable in a number of other ways" he said knowingly. "Great mystery about this boat called Juno".

They left Tory at eighteen hundred hours the following day.

"Darkness will be on us in just over an hour but I just wanted to get away from the King. He's far too clever and perceptive for his own good. We can put in to Sheephaven for the night. We can moor under the monastery" said Devlin.

"I don't think I'll be nipping ashore to get the Brothers to hear my confession" laughed Sean, "it would be far too great a shock for them".

"Doesn't look dangerous" said Joe viewing the explosives.

"Enough for our task" said Devlin.

"Remember we are going for maximum publicity with this one, to show we are still in business".

Early next morning they left the sheltered mooring of Sheephaven and began following the coastline northwards.

"We'll give the big beaches of the North Coast a wide berth" directed Devlin. "It's all windsurfers, forever having to be rescued by the lifeboat or other local craft. The last thing we need is to be involved in some heroic rescue.

CHAPTER 19

Taking advantage of the continuing good weather, Alan and Mike were having their morning coffee on the patio in front of the apartments. Not a breath of air disturbed the stillness. In the clear sky the vapour trails of transatlantic jets hung like heavenly garlands, while out in the bay a flotilla of racing yachts lay becalmed with sails hanging limply.

A scene of tranquillity and peace.

"I'm bored" said Alan.

"You weren't saying that a fortnight ago when they were shooting at you in Donegal", said Mike.

"One forgets the fear but not the excitement".

"Yea, I miss it too" said Mike, "maybe we should see if Claire would like to have lunch" he added hopefully.

"She seems to be seeing a fair bit of Commander Harris".

"Sure he has been divorced twice already" said Mike, totally oblivious to his own situation.

"What does she see in him anyway?"

"How about, youth, good looks, wealth" said Alan.

"Well, apart from that".

"I wonder is Sarah still staying with her sister, it was a good idea, brings them closer together and means she'll be able to rest up after the operation to remove the implants. I hope things go well with her and Burns, she could do with a little bit of TLC, although mind you Burns has a hard, nasty side to him".

"What did you do in the past when you got bored?" asked Alan.

"Usually changed the car, wife, girlfriend or business".

"Sounds hellishly expensive".

"It was. Why don't you change the old Mercedes – that would give you a lift?"

"To what"

"One of those SLK sports cars, I quite fancy myself in one of those touring North Down in the summer months with the hood down".

"Do you not think we're a bit old for such a car", said Alan.

"Nonsense, 70 is the new 40" replied Mike, "besides it would be very appropriate for Holmes and Watson. We could have it in silver or maybe black would be better".

Just then one of the neighbours breezed over.

"Haven't seen much of you about recently, have you been away?"

"Few days in Donegal a couple of weeks ago".

"Donegal is a bit dead for me specially at this time of the year" said the neighbour.

"We were nearly too dead for it" retorted Mike.

The neighbour moved away looking puzzled. "Haven't seen any of your vans recently" he said over his shoulder as he left them, "certainly makes for easier parking when they are not here".

Mike was about to retort when Alan laid a hand on his shoulder, "Don't rise to the bait" he said, "it's not worth it. They are just curious about the life you lead"

"They would certainly be surprised if they knew of the events in Donegal".

Claire and Jack Harris did not really have a lot in common. Whilst she was interested in music, ballet and philosophy, his interest ran more to golf, rugby and trashy novels. However, their joint experiences over the previous few weeks had given them a common base to focus on, and it was sufficient to enable them to meet socially on a few occasions, although the differences between them remained wide.

Reluctantly, Claire had repeatedly listened to him relate the details of his two divorces and became more alarmed as he refused to accept even a small share of the blame for the collapse of these relationships. He seemed to be out of touch, not only with other people's feelings but also his own. He was domineering and into control, but he refused to accept this as part of his nature. He saw himself as a stern but fair father to the two children from his first marriage, and as a concerned husband and provider to his two ex-wives who, in his opinion, had not been able to put up with the long hours and erratic shifts he worked.

'Too much education needed there' thought Claire, 'I'm far too old and comfortable to begin such a training process which would probably be doomed to failure anyway'. However, she planned to see what he was like in bed before coming to any final conclusions.

From Harris' perspective Claire was an interesting, attractive woman who was easy to talk to although she did need putting to rights on certain matters. In his opinion, she was too innocent, too idealistic on many matters and was too trusting of people. Still, in his company he had no doubt his views would prevail as she recognised his wealth of experience and his knowledge of people and the world.

He couldn't understand why she refused to accompany him to his golf club. O.K. she didn't play, but at least she could socialise and meet some of his friends. Just shy, he supposed, but that would cure in time.

In the meantime his thoughts were turning to seduction. That was part of the equation still missing. Physically she was very attractive to him, but there was a certain chill which indicated that the issue of sex was very much in her court and on her terms.

Still, he never had trouble or complaints about that area in the past and was certain that his performance would be well up to standard. As he thought about it, he began to get aroused and considered, like a teenager, nipping off to the toilets, but remembering he was a commander in Counter Terrorist Command decided against it.

He decided instead to invite her out to dinner, although not to the Golf Club!

On their return from Donegal, Sarah had decided to accept Claire's invitation to stay with her for a few weeks. It wasn't that she was scared to stay on her own, but rather after the trauma she had suffered,she felt in need of some comfort.

The small toe, or rather what was left of it, had become infected and it was decided not to remove the implants until it had healed. In the meantime Frank Burns had been very solicitous and attentive, not, she accepted, in any sleazy way, but rather she would describe it as professional concern. The events which had befallen her weighed heavily on his shoulders as he took full blame. His colleagues told him to wise up, MI5 and emotions did not run together. He was only doing his job in the most efficient way he knew. He understood their logic but could not accept it in the circumstances. He had a real liking and respect for the damaged, vulnerable individual that was Sarah and blamed himself for bringing even more trouble and pain into her life.

Sarah, for her part, could not help but bear a bit of a grudge. Frank had spooked her into flight without which none of this would have happened. It was still unclear how the loss of her toe would affect her walking but she reckoned it was an amputation she could well have done without. As for the implants, the memory device implanted in her breast had been read by the special machine designed to do this, but she now felt their presence to be really intrusive, even to the extent of hurting. She realised that this was largely psychological because over the previous four years she had never been aware of their presence but she couldn't wait to get rid of this equipment which her body now clearly considered alien.

Still, she had to admit, there was something attractive about Frank. The soft and hard together, the caring side coupled with a very different, almost brutal, and certainly dangerous violent side, appealed to her as it had done so many times since her youth. But then as she reflected, it had never turned out happily for her, the only exception being Tom, and his harsh side seldom revealed itself. Still, she thought it interesting that they were both in the same line of work. She reckoned she had plenty of time to consider her position since, although he had asked to take her to dinner, he had said not until the implants were removed and she had recovered.

In the meantime, he was a regular caller.

CHAPTER 20

"It's nice to see you", said Claire to Alan and Mike as they stood on her door step. "but you should have telephoned".

"We were just passing and wanted to check that you were alright" Mike said.

"If it's not convenient don't worry" said Alan.

"No, no it's just a surprise, come in, Sarah is here as well".

They were only seated when the door bell went.

A voice they recognised drifted in from the hall. "I hope you don't mind but I got your address from the police. I've been so worried since your sister went missing, then I heard she had been found and was staying with you. I was so relieved I just had to see her and find out how she's keeping. I do hope you don't mind". Lily Platt strode into the room.

"Oh, you're here" she said to Mike and Alan obviously puzzled and confused but, with curiosity in the ascendancy she advanced on Sarah, arms outstretched.

"I'm so glad to see you dear, I've been so worried".

"That's kind of you Mrs... Mrs".....

"Platt dear, Lily Platt, your neighbour. You poor dear you must be so tired and confused. Tell me all about it".

"All about what?" said Sarah.

"Well, whatever happened to you?" said Lily, her confidence ebbing away. "I didn't know you knew the family", she commented turning to Mike and Alan.

Claire intervened. "These are old friends who have given up their afternoon to visit us" .

Lily got the message. "Of course dear, I must be on my way. My husband is waiting outside in his taxi, we were just passing and I wanted to make sure you were alright but sure I'll hear all about it when you get home".

"I'll see you out" said Sarah, limping to the door.

"Sore foot dear, don't worry we'll have a wee cup of tea and a nice long chat when you get home. I know you must be dying to tell me the whole story".

Sarah returned to the lounge. "I wonder could I claim compensation to move house. It looks like a necessity for my sanity!".

"Big numbers just passing by this afternoon".

Mike and Alan looked embarrassed.

"Oh, I don't mean you, I'm only joking! Tea or coffee?"

The door bell went again.

This time Commander Harris was ushered into the room. He also was surprised and none too pleased to see Mike and Alan.

"You two old guys still alive" he said, none too pleasantly.

"Sorry to disappoint you" said Mike.

"How is business these days?" remarked Harris knowingly. Mike subsided.

"Now Jack will you have tea or coffee?" asked Claire.

"Well, we're safer and more comfortable here than we were in Donegal" said Alan. They were sitting in the lounge, tea cups carefully balanced, looking like a group of Presbyterian Church elders. Polite conversation was conducted largely between Claire and Alan. Mike and Harris glowered at each other while Sarah seemed largely lost in thought.

"Was there anything else you wanted"? asked Claire, posing the question to Jack Harris after the normal questions of concern had been asked and answered.

"I was going to ring" said Harris "but I just happened to be passing".

"Yet another" said Sarah. Harris looked puzzled.

"I was wanting to invite you to dinner" said Harris, looking at Claire.

"That's exceptionally generous of you" said Mike quickly, "but you can't stand for all of us, we will all pay our own way".

"Of course we will" chorused Alan and Sarah with Claire nodding.

Harris looked balefully and threateningly at Mike who beamed back. "I'll get my secretary to arrange it" he said "Claire, may I have a private word".

At the door Harris explained that the invitation had been intended only for her.

"I'm sorry, but I didn't realise" she said, "What about a drink tomorrow night?" suggested Harris.

"I'm sure that would be nice" she said.

"Meet you about 8. 00 pm in the Regent Hotel?"he said.

Back in the house, Mike and Alan were talking to Sarah.

"They kept me in hospital for 3 days but they brought in a portable scanning device which was able to read the memory chip. They now have the whole conversation on transcript; voices, individuals, all recorded and identified. Frank Burns tells me the descriptions have been circulated. Two of the leadership team have already been picked up. No sign of the top men however. Mind you the chances are they were on the Juno when she went down although I have a bad feeling about it".

"What"? said Mike, "you are worried about those animals, the bringers of death and destruction, they cut off your toe, how could you have any sympathy for them?"

"No,no, I didn't mean that, I just have a 6th sense that maybe they didn't get blown up or drowned. I can't explain it. It's just something I feel, and they didn't find any bodies or wreckage".

"The strength of the explosion maybe destroyed everything" suggested Alan.

"I hope so, but as I say I just have a feeling".

"We used to think Sarah was psychic when she was a child" said Claire coming back into the room. "She used to have these feelings which were often right".

"Let's hope this time she's wrong".

"I'll be happier when these implants are out, they think that they may be able to operate next week".

"It's time we were on our way" said Alan.

"If you need anything just ring me" said Mike to Claire. She smiled. "Last time you said that, you got more than you bargained for".

"I feel unsettled" complained Mike on the way home. "I'd like to do something different"'

"Tell you what" said Alan, "since you suggested that I change the car I've been in the notion of checking out some car dealers, we could do that tomorrow".

"Good idea Watson and I'll wear a suit. Always looks better in these posh garages".

A love of cars was a shared passion between the two men and a trip to Belfast to look around car showrooms was like taking a couple of eight year olds on a visit to a toyshop.

On the road to Belfast they once again had to run the gauntlet of the cones but Mike remained surprisingly placid.

"Think I'll complain to my local councillor" he said "wouldn't be so bad if there was actually work going on but nothing ever seems to be happening".

The majority of the prestige car dealers were all conveniently located in the same area. Mercedes sat cheek to jowl with BMW, Saab, Porsche, Volvo, Audi, VW, Jaguar, Aston Martin, Ferrari, Lexus, Land Rover and Alfa Romeo.

The showrooms were all surprisingly similar in layout. High gloss tiles, chrome fittings, huge glass areas and all with a budding supermodel as receptionists – all of whom appeared to be cloned from the same blonde, leggy, pencil- skirted original. The clones also came with two voices, one for greeting customers and for telephone use, the other for any mechanic or blue collared worker who dared to venture into their domain. Part of that domain in each showroom comprised a bijoux food provision. Impossibly small sandwiches and tiny pastries nestled under glass covers beside a coffee machine. Small tables, chairs, artificial trees and shrubs completed the pavement café image. It was, Alan noted, described as a complimentary service for customers, at least they didn't call it free.

"We need to plan our day" said Mike. "I vote we have breakfast with BMW, morning coffee with Porsche, lunch with Mercedes and afternoon tea with Saab, depending of course on who has the best food".

It was of course cars which were the main attraction.

"Can I help you gentlemen?" enquired a smooth young salesman.

"You haven't got a brother who's a hotel manager in Donegal by any chance?" asked Mike.

Alan was getting worried, he knew the warning signs. Thank God, he thought, that no alcohol was available.

"That's an insulting figure to offer my friend for his fine car" said Mike, after the salesman had given the old Mercedes a cursory inspection.

"I'm sorry Sir, but it is 20 years old, we would have to move it on through the trade".

"I won't stand here and let him be insulted. Come along my friend" he said, grabbing Alan by the arm.

The salesman looked shocked – as did Alan.

"My father can be difficult at times", he said apologetically as they left.

"What was that about?" enquired Alan when they returned to the car.

"Didn't like the cars, the salesman or the showroom".

"I have an idea" said Alan. "Let's adopt different persona for each showroom".

"Good idea Watson. What about being eccentric French millionaires?"

"Bonjour, nous sommes intereste dans une voiture. Mon ami conduit un vieux Mercedes".

"C'est vrai mon ami, l'automobile est tres belle".

"Combien de la monnai donnez vous pour la voiture belle?"

The young salesman looked surprised and wary. "Are you French?" he asked.

"Mai oui, nous sommes francai s, nous habite une grande chateau a Paris. Nous sommes millionaires eccentric. Vous comprenez?"

"I'm sorry I don't speak French very well. Pardon messieurs mai je ne parle francais, cependant notre directeur est Francais. Attends moi s'il vous plait. Je lui ai envoye un message et il va parler avec vous".

He walked over to reception and picked up the phone.

"Fuck me" said Mike. " someone can actually speak the bloody language. "Let's get out of here". They headed for the door.

"Nous sommes allez a la car park pour voir les voitures seconde main". Said Alan to the surprised young salesman.

"That could have been a bit embarrassing" said Alan. "These visits aren't going too well".

"Upwards and onwards" said Mike.

The next showroom was launching a new car and a drinks reception was well underway.

"Good show" said Mike.

'Perhaps this is not a good idea' thought Alan.

"Would you care to sign the register of interests gentlemen?" said an overdressed salesman.

"Pleased to" replied Mike pushing Alan towards the open address book. "I will sign after you".

"So glad you could make it, your Lordship", simpered the salesman a few minutes later. "Sharon, bring over some champagne for Lord Castleford and his friend".

'What the hell's going on', thought Alan and went over to the register where, unmistakably in Mike's handwriting was the name Lord Castleford. He went back over to Mike.

"What the fuck is this about" he asked angrily, "you can't go round impersonating real people"!

"I'm not. I bought the title twenty years ago when I was drunk, of course. I used to use it for business but haven't actually used it since I came back from Germany".

"Well, I'll be damned", said Alan.

"Your champagne your Lordship" said the young receptionist with eyes only for Mike.

"Oh yes", he whispered to Alan. "Forgot to say – it's also great for pulling the birds"!

"Would you like to take a test drive your Lordship?"

"No thanks, I buy a car on looks and comfort. My man here does all the driving for me. I'll take another glass of champagne though – you shouldn't drink anymore Watson since you have to drive, I'll drink yours instead".

"Certainly your Lordship, anything you say, take a seat and I'll have a bottle of champagne sent over" said a new arrival who turned out to be the sales manager.

"Was I very badly behaved?" asked Mike three hours later as he slumped in the front seat of the Mercedes. "By the way, the car still stinks of sheepdip – no wonder we couldn't get a good price on it".

"I've seen you worse. They did feed you a lot of drink and you did appear to them to be very keen on the car".

"I didn't buy it – did I?"

"Don't know – you went upstairs to an office with them at one time".

"I don't remember that".

"It was just after you demonstrated your skill at Greek dancing and trod heavily on the sales manager's foot. He thought it might be broken. Certainly he went off to casualty".

"I really don't remember".

"I'm not surprised. You fell asleep in the backseat of the new model they were launching. They couldn't get you wakened and when they did you wouldn't get out".

"I wasn't sick, was I?"

"Only slightly, in one of the big tubs holding a tree".

"What were you doing?"

"I'm just the servant – remember? I know my place. The staff were very good to you and gave you coffee to help sober you up. As we were leaving they said they would try to speed up delivery – whatever that means. All the details are in that envelope on the back seat".

"Dear God what have I done", groaned Mike.

CHAPTER 21

At the Regent Hotel the next evening Claire was about 10 minutes late. She had not taken any particular care in dressing although she had chosen flimsy red underwear, just in case. Her jeans were a neat fit and a silk blouse gaped just enough to be interesting. Her hair, recently cut, was, she knew, sitting well.

She strode confidently into the bar. Jack Harris got to his feet and greeted her with a kiss to her cheek. Conversation was a bit strained although it became easier as the contents of a bottle of house wine became less.

"So you see both wives had a lot in common, they found it difficult to cope with the shift patterns, the anti-social hours, the uncertainty, and the fear.

The first, Maureen, was very withdrawn and didn't like going out – not even to the golf club, which meant that since I had to be there as Vice-Captain, I was usually alone which of course made temptation harder to resist".

Claire's eyes began to glaze over.

"I was never really unfaithful" went on Jack, "just the odd little fling, but really we weren't compatible and when she suggested divorce I wasn't surprised. Of course, she took the house and the children opted to stay with the house. They were poisoned against me by their mother, even though I was the one who put food on the table, paid their school fees and gave them pocket money. They wouldn't give me the time of day. I still have little to do with them.

"Second wife was Jane. She already had three sons and didn't want more children. The boys were a bit of a handful. They drifted between her and her ex-husband and I had to use all my influence to keep them out of the courts. Things weren't helped by Jane's drink problem – something she had kept hidden from me. She was always drinking orange juice – part of her five-a-day she said. What I didn't realise was that from breakfast on it was laced with vodka. Of course no-one can live with a drunk. Apart from that, she was a bit too friendly with some of the male neighbours who took advantage of her little weaknesses. Eventually I couldn't stand it any longer and divorced her. Another house gone. Next time instead of getting married again, I'm just going to find a woman I don't like and give her a house"!

"I think someone came up with that quote before you" said Claire. "Look I don't mean to be rude, but can we change the topic, we've been over this endless times".

"Sorry" he said. "It just bugs me and you're so easy to talk to".

A rather uneasy silence followed. Claire, in an effort to banish her embarrassment, rather too quickly finished the bottle of Merlot.

"Would you like to move on to a club?" asked Jack. "There's a folk music group in Shepperd's Bar just up Main Street".

"That's a good idea" responded Claire, aware that the conversation was becoming strained again.

The folk group was very average and the cultivated mid-western accents didn't help. When Claire considered the musical talent of her own sons, there was no comparison with this second rate group. She considered her sons for a moment. She didn't see much of them any longer. University in England had created a gulf, nothing she could put her finger on, but their lives were now focussed on their careers. They came home frequently but when they got steady girlfriends she reckoned she'd see even less of them. Sad, but what could she do?.

The folk music, poor though it was, at least meant she didn't have to converse much. Somewhat to her surprise she had moved from wine to Guinness, which was not a particularly good idea. The mixture tended to go to her head quickly and Jack Harris was generously keeping her well supplied. She didn't know why she had changed her choice of drink – perhaps it was something to do with the folk music.

She sat back and observed Jack. In front of her she saw a tall, middle aged, fit man with greying hair, dressed in a conventional blue suit worn over a dark navy T-shirt. He had good strong features she had to admit, although his eyes seemed to lack in colour and brightness, a sort of watery grey. 'And they say the eyes are the windows on the soul', she thought.

It was always when drinking Guinness that she was tempted to smoke, somehow the two always went together in her mind, but again she realised that to smoke meant going out into the cold dark night. She remained amazed that the Irish had taken so easily to the smoking ban.

The bar was crowded, mostly with young people who were lowering the drink as if it was going out of fashion. They were all good humoured and she was aware that with the dim light hiding her features but not her slim figure, a few young studs were fancying their chances.

She wondered how Jack would take that. Not well she guessed. She was more conscious than ever of how little they had in common and would have found the evening tedious had it not been for the music to minimise the need for conversation, which all too often simply became polite arguments.

The combination of wine and Guinness had, however, gone to her head, and when Jack caressed her hand she made no objection. 'Let's see where it leads' she thought.

Where it led to was back to the Regent Hotel...Jack with, she thought, the assurance of someone who had done this before, went over to reception and booked a room for the night. She remained in the background looking at a local events poster, looking but not reading because she was damned if she was going to put her glasses on!

Jack came over to her. "Room 12" he said, taking her arm for a very unsteady climb up the stairs and along the first floor corridor to Room 12. Something about the whole scenario struck her as being incredibly funny and she had to concentrate hard to avoid a fit of the giggles, which she reckoned, wouldn't do much for the romantic mood Jack was intent on creating.

It took a bit of fumbling with the key to get the door open, but eventually they stepped into a dark room which could have been in any hotel, anywhere in the world.

The door locked, he took her in his arms and held her tightly.

"I really fancy you" he said.

"I can feel you do" said Claire playfully as she removed her blouse.

The alcohol prevented any feelings of shyness and Jack stretched out on the large bed, viewing appreciatively her naked body. She also ran her eyes up and down his. 'Nice dick' she thought as she straddled him. Not too bad for a late middle aged couple. 'Ahh...that's a bit nice' she thought as she altered her position.

Suddenly her attention began to wander and she slipped out and lay on her back. Jack took this as encouragement and caressing her breast entered her again.

She lay back looking at the marks and cracks on the ceiling. "Hmm", she whispered, hoping to sound appreciative, but her mind was elsewhere. Jack suddenly realised something was not right and immediately lost his erection.

"What's wrong?" he asked.

"Nothing" she said, "it's just been a long time since I had sex".

"Well what are you thinking about" he continued.

And that as far as she was concerned, that was it!

"Was it something I did or said?"

"No, it has nothing to do with you" she said. "It's me. The surroundings, the atmosphere have to be right, it has to happen in the mind before it gets to the body. It's not your fault, it's just the way I am. I'm sorry".

It was with some degree of embarrassment that they walked down the stairs. Jack quickly settled the bill and hailed a taxi. It was about 4.00 am but there was still life about.

"Lend us a fiver mister" shouted a none too happy young drunk, or let's share your taxi with us" he went on. Harris flipped his warrant card.

"Fuck off" he said.

They had a quiet journey back to Claire's house. "I won't invite you in" she said, "thank you for the evening". Harris just smiled.

The next morning dawned bright and fair, which was more than could be said for Claire who, finding her sister awake when she arrived home after 4.00 a.m. in the morning, opened another bottle of wine and sat on the edge of her bed discussing men, sex and ageing until 7.00 a.m.

Exactly two hours later, Alan poured out tea for Mike and himself. They were sitting basking in the early morning sun on the patio overlooking the Marina. They sat without speaking watching the passage of boats entering and leaving the harbour. It was quite a busy harbour, for apart from the hundreds of pleasure craft in the Marina, there were also about twenty fishing boats ranging in size from quite tiny to three large boats capable of reaching the Icelandic fishing grounds.

Alan's attention was drawn to a blue fishing boat coming slowly around to the harbour mouth.

"That boat's a bit like what the Juno was" he commented.

Mike stuck his head out from behind the Daily Mirror, "wrong colour" he stated.

"Yes, it's the basic design that is the same, that is what jogged my memory".

On board the Juno, now bearing the name 'Amethyst' Mr Devlin gave the directions. "We'll refuel, then tie up at one of the visitor moorings" he said. "We need some basic items like batteries and, of course, food".

"Is it not risky to go ashore?" asked Joe.

"We must be careful" said Francis, "but no-one knows me here and I can maintain a German accent. Besides, I won't be ashore very long!"

"Where are you going?" Claire asked her sister.

"I thought I would like to take a walk through TK MAX" said Sarah.

"I quite fancy that as well but really my head is too sore".

"No problem, I'll take the bus to the town centre".

Conscious of her injured foot, Sarah stepped down from the bus very carefully. It was a short walk to the store but she took it very gently. She really should have used the crutch the hospital had sent her home with, but pride forbade it.

As with so many town centres, Bangor played host to a multitude of offices, Banks, Building Societies and Charity Shops. Little really to attract the serious shopper! Passing the Pound Shop she considered going in but, realising her love of a bargain, she knew she would come out with a bag full of pruck she didn't need. Instead she went into a local newsagents and bought a magazine and a national paper.

She spent a good half hour in TK MAX but items in her size she did not want and items she did want were not in her size.

Still, it had taken her out of the house and given her a little bit of exercise. She again considered the Pound Shop and was on the point of entering when she felt she was going to faint. The reason for her loss of blood pressure was standing at the checkout with a box of batteries in his hand. It was Francis from Juno.

She stood petrified, rooted to the spot. The horror of what he had done to her and what he represented, temporarily paralyzed her. Then, almost in slow motion she saw him turn away from the check out and walk towards the door. Desperately she dodged behind a group of gossiping mothers, their offspring in buggies, which effectively blocked the footpath. Francis had to step on to the road to pass and, keeping his eye on the traffic, he didn't notice her.

Frantically she searched her handbag for her new mobile which she had bought on her return from Donegal. Of course she wasn't familiar with it, so it seemed to take an age to connect with her sister.

"Claire you must come and get me. Don't ask, just get down here. I'll wait for you at the bottom of Main Street".

Claire was slower off the mark than usual but even so 20 minutes later she'd picked up her sister and taken her to a nearby coffee shop.

"I couldn't believe it" said Sarah, visibly shaken. "He was just standing there, I thought I was hallucinating. I really thought I was going mental, seeing images that didn't exist. And I was so scared".

"Are you quite sure it was him?" asked Claire. "I mean I don't doubt your word but as far as we know he's at the bottom of the Atlantic".

"You remember I had a feeling about it? I just felt something was wrong".

"We must inform the police but I really don't want to talk to

Jack Harris so soon after last night".

"I'll ring Frank Burns".

She got through to Burns immediately. "Go home and stay there" he said. "I'll be along within the hour".

As they left the coffee shop they were hailed from across the street. Mike and Alan waved over and crossed over to them.

"Ladies, you look as if you've just had a fright, surely prices aren't rising that quickly?" said Mike.

"She's just seen Francis" said Claire.

"Francis who?"

"From the boat, the men in the pub. Conflict's leaders".

"My God" said Alan "so the Juno didn't go down".

"We've just informed Frank Burns" said Claire.

"You go home and wait for Burns. I've an idea. If I come up with anything I will let you know. Get Burns to ring me".

"What do we do?" asked Mike.

"Remember the boat this morning that reminded me of Juno?"

"Wrong colour".

"Wrong colour but right boat, it's been repainted and camouflaged".

"Where is it now, down in the Marina?"

"Unless it's already been moved".

"Let's go and see if it's still there".

The Marina was protected by water on one side and barred gates on the land side. However, Mike knew the warden on duty and he let them in.

"Just want to check on a boat for sale" said Mike.

They strolled down the sloping gangway.

"Watch they don't see us" said Alan, "or they might flee".

"They might take us out first" said Mike. His phone went.

"Frank" he said. "Will do".

"Burns wants us, if we can, to identify the boat, then back off, but not to let ourselves be seen".

They walked towards the visitors' moorings. As they approached the 'Amethyst' it was quite clear to them, since they knew the boat well, that it was the Juno in camouflage. Suddenly there was movement on deck. The two men were totally exposed on the walkway.

"Follow me" said Mike, stepping down into the well of a large seagoing yacht. He addressed two surprised crew members in Swedish.

A period of confusion followed.

"So you are not Swedish and didn't ask for the Swedish deputy consul?" Mike said pointing at Alan. No one was now on the deck of Juno.

"Well, sorry about the mistake" said Mike, "we must've got the wrong boat".

"Tak sa mycket" said Alan, using the only Swedish he knew.

Burns was waiting for them at the gates of the Marina.

"Well".

"It's the Juno in disguise" said Alan. "No doubt about it".

Burns offered to drive them back to the apartments.

"What the hell are they doing here? We must get observation organised".

"Why not go in and arrest them?"

"We need to know what they're up to. They'll have changed their original plans".

"I'll put the boat under constant surveillance. In the meantime just stay off side, I'll get the Special Boat Service down".

"We can keep an eye on it from the balcony of the apartments" said Alan.

"Don't be getting involved"

"She's on the move", cried Alan, as the boat slowly left the mooring and nosed its way towards the harbour mouth.

"What, we've nothing in place yet. What direction's she heading for?"

"Could be over to the Co Antrim side".

"The oil and gas terminals".

"They'll not let her near them. She's turning up the Lough. I know, I'll get the bicycle out and follow along the coastal path behind her", said Alan.

"Can you still ride a bike?" said Burns.

Alan cycled along the coastal path but didn't have to go far. At the first sandy beach, the 'Amethyst' moored off and the tender came ashore. From his hidden vantage point Alan could see bags of sand being filled and dumped in the tender. 'Very odd' he thought.

When the tender was back on board the boat made no effort to move but remained peacefully moored.

On board there was great glee. "Is this our lucky day or not" said Devlin.

"Couldn't have played into our hands better" said Francis.

"I couldn't believe our luck when I saw in the paper Francis brought back that tomorrow sees the Topping Out ceremony for the Titanic centre, and who are doing the honours but the First and Deputy First Ministers! With a bit of luck we'll get both of them. Two for the price of one".

"Come back Alan" said Burns on the phone. "We'll have people in place shortly".

The watchers took up their positions by the back of the bay and prepared for a cold dark night.

The Juno sat easily at anchor, her riding lights cutting through the darkness.

Towards dawn as the sky started to lighten, the watchers were in for a surprise. The boat had vanished. In its place were the riding lights fixed to buoys, which in turn were moored by long ropes tied to sand bags dropped to the seabed.

Also attached to one of the buoys was a small radio playing away which the watchers had taken as proof of life on board.

When he was awakened with the news, Burns was furious. It would take some time to organise a helicopter search and more than that, he would have to admit to having lost one large fishing boat in the middle of the night. His watchers got the rough end of his tongue even though it was really his fault that they'd not been equipped with night vision glasses.

"She'll have a six hour start on us" said Burns to Harris over the telephone. "Bloody watchers saw nothing. Fair enough, it was a dark, wet night but even so, I don't see how they could've missed her leaving. Mind you, it was a clever idea to fix that radio to one of the buoys. The noise lulled the watchers into a false sense of confidence and security. With her two diesels at full power she could be up to 120 miles away. They could be in the Clyde, amongst the western Isles, Dublin, Liverpool or heading for St George's Channel en route to France. I suppose they could even have gone back to Donegal, although I don't see that as a possibility. I think we should send the chopper over to the Clyde first – although I'm only going on a hunch. They could be anywhere. Even worse, I'll have to let Harris know what has happened. "

"Well they obviously have something planned or they wouldn't have left so secretly", said Harris, "you must be really incensed about it. Still it could happen to anyone" he said.

Burns fumed inwardly as he imagined the smile on Harris's face.

CHAPTER 22

"Tell me again why we got an invitation".

"Because it used to come under a Department in the Civil Service I was in charge of" explained Alan as he struggled to put in his top shirt button and make up his tie.

"And what's a topping out ceremony?"

"It's a ceremony to mark the outside finishing of a building, before they go on and fit out the inside".

"Will there be any drink at it?"

"Sure to be" said Alan.

Traffic was slack so they made it to the Titanic Quarter with plenty of time to spare. They decided to walk around the outside of the huge prow like structure designed to create an image of the Titanic.

"Not much of the old shipyard left apart from the two huge cranes" observed Mike.

"They have started to build wind turbines further down the river" said Alan. "They were always very adaptable, building oil rigs and bridges as well as ship repairs, but it's sad they don't actually build ships any longer". The huge paint shop was still standing in the middle of a vast demolished area.

"They are using the old paint shop as a film set for various blockbuster movies. Apparently the Americans are queuing up to use it. A good money spinner".

"What's that ship down there, just past the paint shop?" asked Mike.

"That's HMS Caroline, the oldest warship from WW1 still afloat".

"That would make a fine tourist attraction when you think of HMS Belfast and the popularity it has achieved moored in the Thames, why not the same with HMS Caroline?"

"I want to stand on the slipway on which Titanic was built" said Mike.

"The actual slip is no longer there but I can show you exactly where it was" said Alan.

The two men made their way around the back of the platform erected for the topping out ceremony. This ceremony wasn't taking place on the top of the building which was usual, but because of the design, safe access to the pinnacle wasn't possible, so the final section of roof was going to be put in place by a crane controlled remotely from the platform.

They walked over to the river bank.

"So this is the exact spot where Titanic stood before being launched?" asked Mike.

"Sure is, this was where the shipway was and over there is where – My God! My God!".

"What is it", asked Mike. "You're not having a heart attack are you?"

"Look there" said Alan, and there was the 'Amethyst'/'Juno', neatly tied up to the far dock.

"Ring Burns" said Mike.

"I'm already doing that" said Alan hitting the speed dial.

"Frank, we're at the Titanic Centre and the Juno is tied up opposite, no sign of life. Right, right, O. K. Burns says he'll be here as soon as possible. In the meantime we just keep watch".

Within twenty minutes Burns was standing beside them.

"They are going to delay the ceremony for half an hour to do another sweep for bombs. Everything was checked yesterday but

Juno hadn't been here then. There is a real danger that bombs could have been planted during the night. How the hell the Harbour Police missed her arrival I don't know. Where the bombs are is anyone's guess. They don't have the resources to make a large bomb, so we must assume they're using a number of small devices to create confusion and fear and guarantee world wide publicity. There's no chance of them getting explosives anywhere near the platform party so the First and Deputy First Minister are safe enough. The Juno's being searched at present, three marksmen are in position but something is missing. It's also a bit ironical that they've chosen to dock right beside the Police Authority building".

"Maybe that's their target" said Mike.

"Unlikely", replied Burns, "that would require something like a car bomb and wouldn't have the same world wide publicity angle". He listened to his earpiece. Three small bombs found around perimeter of the site, no attempt to hide them and no attempt to break into the site.

"They must've found security too tight" said Mike.

"We're missing something" said Alan.

More information was being relayed to Burns through his earpiece. "What" he said suddenly into his microphone, "say again". "Right. Commander Harris and his team are responsible for ground security, let them know and get a helicopter in the air, then get back to me".

"What's happening" asked Mike.

"When they searched the Juno, they found nothing of note except for a piece of cardboard, a wrapper with 416 Barrett 10. 5 × 83 printed on it, which someone had let fall under the table".

"So" said Mike.

"I get it" said Alan, "That's sniper ammunition".

"Go to the top of the class. That is the ammo for the Barrett Sniping rifle. The explosives are now only a distraction, they are going to try to hit the First and Deputy First Ministers as they perform the Topping Out ceremony, but where are they going to hit from?" He spoke to his own marksmen and to the observer in the helicopter. The redevelopment of the old shipyard and docks area meant that the site was overlooked by dozens of high rise office and apartment blocks. The ones closest had already been checked during the previous two days, but there were so many more.

Sean Brennan lay motionless on the top of the Police Authority Building. He was well covered and well camouflaged from above and below and had a clear view down the Barrett's telescopic site of the platform across the river where the ceremony would soon take place. He'd been there since 6.00 am.

The climb up the outside of the building had been surprisingly easy even in darkness. The balconies provided easy grip for the light grappling irons and ropes. They had opted for the Police Authority building partly because they knew it had already been checked out and also the publicity value of the hit being made from the very building from which security policy emanated.

He was quite comfortable and relaxed, his only problem being he couldn't move to take a pee, so he had to do it where he was lying. However, the absorbent padding he'd packed into his crotch absorbed most of it. Besides it did not matter much. He'd no escape route planned. After he'd killed his two targets, he would be either shot or arrested. They would identify very quickly where the bullets came from and, with the helicopter hovering above, escape would be impossible. It didn't worry him. If he was shot he'd be a martyr like the hunger strikers or other volunteers killed in action. If arrested, he'd savour being a hero.

He cradled the Barrett to his shoulder. For such a weapon the range was short and he was an accurate shot. He had yet to kill a human being but he knew he was quite capable of it, and the best shot in the organisation.

The platform party for the Topping Out ceremony was coming into view, surrounded by security men pushing the press and TV reporters to one side. There was, he noticed, a very strong police presence, except he thought, 'They are in the wrong place'!

"Don't do it Sean, it's the wrong way" said a voice behind him.

Sean twisted around, amazed to see Joe standing training a revolver on him. "Joe, what are you doing here?".

"Trying to prevent you doing something which would turn the clock back".

"But Joe, you were always with us, right from the start".

"No, I was always with PIRA supporting the Sinn Fein position. I was asked by them to join Conflict and report on their activities. We indulged you. Do you honestly think we didn't know you'd helped yourselves to one of our small, partially decommissioned arms dumps in Donegal? However, now we feel that Conflict has gone too far. Roll away from the rifle".

"Are you working with the Brits in this?" demanded Sean.

"No way, we are working for a united Ireland based on democratic equality. Do you not understand the days for violence are over?"

"You are a traitor to the cause, you're in bed with the Brits" shouted Sean, kicking out at Joe's knee. But, lying in the cramped position for so long had stiffened his joints and slowed his actions, so no contact was made. He then began to draw a small automatic pistol from his waistband.

Joe stepped back, a revolver in hand. "Don't do it", he said, "please see sense".

Sean lifted his automatic and Joe pulled the trigger. A little hole appeared between Sean's eyes which now held a look of amazement and a splash of blood and brain tissue stained the wall behind his head.

From the top of Goliath, one of the two huge shipyard cranes, one of Burns' marksmen saw movement on the roof of the Police Authority building. Through his sniper-scope he viewed a man in his thirties with dark hair, check shirt, black anorak and jeans holding a pistol and looking down at something hidden by the parapet.

His training automatically came into play and he squeezed the trigger.

"Have you met the First and Deputy First Ministers before?" asked Mike.

"Only in the line of business" replied Alan.

"Might be a useful contact to have" said Mike, "I have a new massage parlour opening next week. I wonder would either like to open it".

"Don't push your luck".

"Well, we did help to save their lives, you'd think they would be a bit grateful".

No-one at the Topping Out ceremony, apart from security personnel and the intended targets, had been aware of the drama being played out.

At Belfast's Central Station Mr Devlin and Francis were waiting impatiently for the Enterprise Express to Dublin.

"What a cockup" said Francis.

"I'll make sure someone pays for this" said Mr Devlin. "No-one makes a fool of me and gets away with it. When we get to Dublin we can regroup. We still have friends".

"I want to know what happened to Sean and Joe".

"Probably taken out by a Brit sniper. Someone will pay".

They suddenly found themselves surrounded by six men.

"Gentlemen, could we ask you to accompany us", requested Commander Harris.

"Why are you harassing us"? said Devlin angrily. You know you haven't a shred of evidence to go on, so why play these games?

I wouldn't get too confident, said Harris softly, "We have for a start, the complete record of your planning meeting in the mountain bar."

"But she hadn't......... We couldn't find" .... burst out Francis.

"Be quiet Francis" ordered Devlin.

Harris took pleasure in seeing the fear, now evident in Devlin's eyes.

"We have more than enough evidence to put you away for many years. Oh, and you might like to know, that all your friends from the Donegal meeting are already in custody, apart of course, from those who are dead! Coimhlint is finished"

Devlin's shoulders slumped and he appeared to age instantaneously, it was almost as though he seemed to shrink within his suit. He made no response, standing with his head bowed, as two Police Officers escorted Francis off the platform and towards the waiting cars.

A few minutes later Commander Harris could be seen guiding an elderly gentleman in the same direction.

Two weeks later, Harris, true to his word, did host a small dinner party choosing a venue in Holywood. Burns had managed to get invited along.

"Let's all keep in touch" suggested Mike at the end of the meal.

"It doesn't work like that", said Harris, "people are bound together by current events. A month or two down the line we'll have nothing in common and there is nothing worse than reunions where we talk about the old days".

"I wouldn't be so certain, sometimes good things come out of bad experiences" said Frank Burns looking across at Sarah.

"You are too cynical, Jack" said Claire.

"Yet more criticism" mumbled Harris.

"Well" said Mike on the way home in the taxi, "There you go now, that's that". It certainly been an interesting way to spend a few days in March".

"Very profound as always" said Alan.

"Be a bit dull going back to breakfasts as the highlight of the week".

"Oh, I'm sure we'll get by, besides sure you're going to take up fishing".

"What?" said Mike.

"I thought you expressed a very determined interest in fishing when you were in the Sandlands Hotel?"

"Might rather play golf" said Mike, but what I really think is we should set ourselves up in business as private detectives, what do you say Watson? What could we use as a name?"

"How about 'Achy and Shaky Private Investigations' ".

"Too close to reality, I don't like that at all".

"Certainly has a ring of truth about it" said Alan. "However, what we need is a few hours sleep followed by a hearty breakfast..... whose turn is it to pay?"

"Yours" came the immediate response!